# Kane Richards Must Die

# Kane Richards Must Die

## Shanice Williams

Lands Atlantic
Publishing

Kane Richards Must Die
Published by Lands Atlantic Publishing
www.landsatlantic.com

ISBN 978-0982500521

For Martin,
Regardless of the future,
he was there when I needed him.

# 1. ARRIVAL

## Suzanne

As I drew up to the secluded school building the butterflies started. Everyone here probably knew each other and had their own group of friends. I would be the odd one out. The new girl with the strange accent.

Two weeks ago, my mother's employer sent her to Greece on an extended assignment. She didn't trust me to be home alone, so she sent me to America to live with my Aunt Clacy. At first I was looking forward to spending time in the big U.S. of A. but when I got to school my courses were all screwed up. I thought back to when I first found out.

"What?! . . . this could mess up my graduation," I'd fumed; I had already lived through sixteen years of damn school. I would be finished after this semester if I were back home.

"Well, hopefully it'll all get worked out, it's only for a few months. I wouldn't fret too much," my aunt shrugged. Although she still had her British accent, there was a slight twang starting to form in her voice.

"But I'm nearly seventeen! They're not even transferring all of my credits!" I pouted, folding my arms.

"Well, things are different here, I'm afraid." She patted me on the back and then went to her office, leaving me on my own.

I gave the building another once-over before sighing and pushing myself through the door. There was a small reception area, with a couple of worn, padded leather seats in the left corner and a desk on the right. A chubby brown-haired woman with big glasses peeked up at my entrance and then quickly went back to work. I walked over to her desk and cleared my throat.

"Umm, hi . . . I'm Suranne Williams, I'm meant to be starting here today." I smiled nervously and twirled my hair anxiously waiting for her reply. She looked up and cocked her head to the side slightly.

"British, huh?" She eyed me up and down, curiously. I just smiled and nodded once. By the time she found my paperwork, the bell had rung.

"I'll show you to your first class," she announced and then mumbled something that sounded like "eat you up for breakfast." I sure hoped my hearing was playing tricks on me.

Leaving the small office area, she led me down a hallway that had lockers on each side and doors to various classes.

"Well, class has already started, and you're in . . ." she unfolded my timetable and squinted through her thick spectacles.

"English," she confirmed with a nod, before turning down yet another hallway and stopping outside a door to a class. She handed me the folded paper and sighed, "At the end of the day, come back to the reception and we'll get the rest of your details." Then she opened the door and ushered me in. My heartbeat raced and my stomach did flips as the whole class turned to stare at me.

"Sorry to interrupt, Mr. Case. I have the new student here." She smiled at him adoringly. I frowned as I looked at her beaming face. Looks like someone has a crush, I thought.

"Ahh yes. Suranne, am I correct?" The tall man with mousy brown hair and grey eyes smiled down at me warmly whilst handing me my books.

2

"Umm, yeah, that's me," I murmured sheepishly. A rush of whispers erupted around the room, and when I turned, the whole class seemed to be gazing at me with expressions of curiosity and amusement.

"Well, I'll leave her in your very good, capable hands then, Mr. Case," the reception lady announced before leaving the room.

Mr. Case placed a reassuring hand on my shoulder and led me to a desk at the far right end of the class. The guy sitting next to the empty desk grinned at me as I approached. I smiled back shyly, sat down, and placed my books on the desk.

"Hey, I'm Lawrence."

I turned to him and smiled. Up close, he was much better looking than I'd thought, and as he smiled back at me I could feel my face warming. He had spiky black hair and lightly tanned skin, with blue eyes, and a silver stud in his left ear. He wore a plain navy shirt and jeans with black trainers, which all looked good on him.

Mr. Case called everyone's attention and I turned my head back to the front of the class, but he mentioned something about Shakespeare's Much Ado About Nothing. I had already studied the book two years ago. I sighed and looked down at my hands, twining them absently as he spoke.

Suddenly the bell sounded and everyone bustled about gathering their things. Lawrence stood up next to me and smiled as I rose from my chair.

Mr. Case stopped me as I walked past his desk. "Suranne, if you have any trouble keeping up, just let me know and I'll try and explain everything best as I can."

"Umm, thanks, but I've already studied Shakespeare so, I've kind of done it already."

"Including this play?" Mr. Case asked, raising an eyebrow.

I nodded sheepishly and made an exit. Lawrence was standing outside the door waiting for me.

"What are you doing?" I asked, wondering why he was still there.

He raised his eyebrows innocently and smiled at me. "I was just gonna show you to your next class, didn't want you getting lost," he reassured, motioning with his hand for me to follow.

"Oh, thanks," I mumbled.

Breathing a quiet laugh he changed the subject, asking me about my last school and how long I'd been here as we made our way to the next classroom together. We talked about how different it was here for me, and he smiled when I mentioned that I should be getting ready for college. I felt completely relaxed when talking to him and even started laughing at some of his comments. When we entered our next class, the teacher hadn't arrived, so everyone was chatting. Their attention diverted to Lawrence and me as we sat at our desks. All of a sudden there were crowds of people around us, all speaking at once.

"Hey, you're Suranne right?"

"Hey, I'm Kate."

"What's it like?"

"Do you like it here?"

"I hear you're from London."

"Wow! I've always wanted to go there!"

I stared at the different faces, speechless, not sure which question to answer first.

Lawrence chuckled next to me, "Give her some room guys, she's only been here five minutes."

"Yeah, well it might be our only chance. Kane's in her next class," a girl with long blonde hair said. She looked at me with green eyes and smiled.

I heard Lawrence groan and rub his temples with his hand. What was with that? Kane? Who's he, what did she mean by it may be her only chance?

"Hey, I'm Kate." The blonde spoke again, pulling me from my reverie and shaking my hand.

"Who's Kane?"

I heard a couple of girls from behind Kate sigh dreamily as I mentioned his name and I guessed he must be pretty popular with the ladies.

"Kane Richards is—"

"An asshole, stay away from him," Lawrence interrupted her, sounding irritated.

"Dude, he's your best friend," I heard a guy mutter from behind me before Lawrence shrugged.

"So? Doesn't mean it's not the truth. She should be warned."

"Anyway," Kate interrupted impatiently. She seemed angry at how the conversation had progressed; she grabbed a chair and pulled it up towards our desk.

"Whatever you do, don't engage with him in any form whatsoever," she warned, looking at me severely.

"Yeah, like don't speak to him, don't sit by him or nuthin', 'cause once you're sucked in, then bam, it's too late," Lawrence continued.

Kate nodded at his words and then jabbed a thumb behind her at the two girls, who still seemed to be in a dreamy state.

"Otherwise you end up like them," Kate said, rolling her eyes. The guy behind me, who'd spoken before, chuckled. "Come on you guys, she's new. You know Kane's gonna get his hands on her either way. The fact that she's fresh meat don't help."

I turned to glare at him but he just grinned and winked at me before being punched in the gut by Lawrence. I smiled vindictively and turned back in my seat.

"How will I know which one he is?" I asked, puzzled by how serious they all were, like he was some ax murderer or something.

"Believe me, you'll know," Lawrence muttered next to me, looking sad and frustrated, but I just shrugged and let it go. The teacher came in then and the group dispersed to their desks. Kate was the last to go back to her seat. "I'm in your next class, you can sit next to me," she whispered, then she turned and walked away like the others.

"Won't you be there?" I asked, turning round to face Lawrence. He stared at me before he spoke.

"Yeah, but I'll be with Kane, and he's usually the last one in, although . . ." he paused and stared at me thoughtfully, "when he realises you're in his class he'll probably be there first." He sighed and shook his head infinitesimally, disappointment the main expression on his face.

"Is he some kind of misogynistic womaniser or something?" I whispered to Lawrence. He chuckled darkly. "You could say that," he muttered, ducking his head in his book.

Throughout the lesson I pondered this Kane Richards, wondering what kind of a reputation he had gained for himself and what would happen to me if I got caught up in him. I was nervous as I made my way to my next class. People stared at Kate and me as they walked past, but every time I glanced at her, she just smiled back warmly.

When we arrived, people still stared, smirking and muttering something to their neighbors. Kate sat down, and I went to join her. I decided to ask her a few quick questions of advice before Casanova came into the room.

"What do I do if he talks to me?" I whispered to her. She was texting on her phone and she just shrugged without looking up.

"Ignore him," she said simply.

Right, so I'm to just ignore this guy if he talks to me? I mean, I didn't know about her, but I was brought up knowing that if someone speaks to you, it's generally rude to just ignore them. I tapped my fingers against the desk, watching as the class slowly filled up with students. Even though Lawrence claimed I would know who he was, I wasn't so sure. All the guys seemed pretty normal to me.

Just then the class door opened again and in stepped three guys. One of them was Lawrence. Out of the corner of my eye I saw him staring at me, probably appraising my expression, but at the time, I was completely focused on someone else. On him.

Yes, Lawrence was definitely right. Without a doubt, I knew I was staring Kane Richards in the face.

# 2. MEETING

## Suzanne

No questions asked, Kane Richards was a carving of pure perfection.

He looked about six feet tall and had short dark hair, neatly spiked up in front. His facial features were . . . well . . . indescribable. His high cheekbones and firm jaw line were perfectly symmetrical, and his skin was flawless and tanned.

Like Lawrence, he had a stud in his left ear, but it was bigger, and looked much more appealing on him. His eyes were a very light brown that reminded me of the milkiest of chocolate, and his full red lips were screaming to be kissed. He wore a crisp black shirt that emphasised the perfection of his chest, and dark jeans. As he walked down the aisle of desks towards me, there was a string of enthusiastic greetings upon his approach.

"Morning, Kane."

"Hi, Kane."

"Hey, did you get my message?"

The greetings continued as he walked past them without giving any inclination of a reply. He didn't look at them, didn't speak, he didn't even nod. He just carried on walking, his milky chocolate eyes fixed on mine. He flashed a crooked grin in my direction as I stared at him in awe, my mind barely comprehending the fact that he was getting closer to my desk.

"Oh, great," Kate groaned and ducked her head to write something in her notebook. I decided to follow her example and tore my eyes away from his perfection, doodling on the back of my timetable, but before I knew it, I felt the paper being pushed aside by a set of extremely attractive hands, and as I glanced up, Kane Richards sat down on the side of my desk. A whiff of expensive, mouthwatering cologne swirled up my nose and I nearly choked on the sweetness of his smell. *This was going to be difficult.*

"Suranne Williams, I'm told." My ears rang as his deep and seductive voice hugged the smooth words that slid off his tongue. I stared at him, my eyes wide and locked in his gaze as he arched one thick eyebrow. Before I had the chance to answer, a slender girl in a very revealing vest, with bouncy brunette curls, walked up to Kane and tapped him lightly on the shoulder with two fingers. I recognised her as one of the girls who was dreamily sighing when I mentioned his name in my last class. His eyes never left mine and his eyebrow was still raised

"Yes?" Once again his smooth voice rang in my ears, like he was in song. I looked at the girl who was looking at me with a ferocious jealous glare before eyeing Kane and batting her eyelids ever so slightly.

"So, I had a good time last night?" She said it more like it was a question than a statement in her high reedy voice.

"I'm glad you enjoyed yourself," he said, without the slightest amount of interest. I bit back a smile at his tone, but it couldn't be kept in completely, so I released a very small smirk. He noticed and grinned in response, winking at me ever so slightly. I could definitely understand why the girl next to me had been sighing dreamily. This guy was one hell of a catch. He frowned as he remembered the girl still standing there shifting her weight uncomfortably and turned to glare at her, raising his eyebrows.

"Listen . . . Kelly, can't you see I'm *busy?*" His head inclined slightly in my direction as if to prove his point. The girl's eyes widened, and she blushed, "It's uhh . . . Kerry, actually," she mumbled, her face twisting into a grimace. Kane merely shrugged and turned his glorious face back to me. I peeked quickly behind him to catch Lawrence watching us both, his eyebrows raised and his expression looking worried. I frowned as I remembered our conversation in my last lesson.

*"Is he some kind of misogynistic womaniser or something?"*
*"You could say that."*

Glancing back at Kane and his hypnotic eyes, I raised a brow. "Kane Richards, I presume?" I spoke, trying to keep my voice cold. His eyes widened and he grinned, keeping his stare firmly locked on my face.

"Damn, Lawrence, you didn't tell me her voice was *that* hot," he spoke, his perfectly white teeth shining. My breath caught and I felt the warmth spread over my cheeks and he chuckled gently at my blush.

"Uhh, yeah, she's from London," Lawrence replied, sounding irritated. His voice reminded me once again of our last conversation; I told myself to get a grip and continued to glare at him.

"You have earned quite a reputation here, so I'm told." I kept my voice cool and businesslike as much as possible, but his smile was melting my concentration. His lips turned up into a smirk and he winked at me as his smooth, musical voice caressed my ears.

"I'm the best."

"Hmm," I replied curtly. "They say men with large egos who big themselves up are usually making up for something rather. . . " my eyes roamed down his body and stopped at the belt of his jeans. "Small." I smiled and lifted my head before raising an eyebrow. His eyes tightened ever so slightly and I could see Lawrence trying to fight a smile behind him. The class door opened and a bald man in a tweed jacket walked in, calling the class to order even though the room was silent, everyone turned in their seats, concentrating on Kane and me.

He was still smiling, and suddenly leaned in closer, so that our faces were inches apart. My breathing sped as I smelled his sweet cologne. I could almost taste it on my tongue and I instantly wanted more. Unconsciously, I leaned my head a tiny fraction in his direction, and he chuckled before sliding off the desk.

"She wants me," I heard him murmur to one of his friends as he approached his own desk and gracefully sat down. My jaw dropped and I stared after him with narrowed eyes, feeling both frustrated and flustered.

So *this* was Kane Richards.

# 3. FAVOUR

## Suranne

"What the *hell* was that?!" Kate asked leaning against her locker as I put my books in the one newly allocated to me. The locker door was obscuring her face so I couldn't see her expression, but she sounded annoyed.

"What?" I asked innocently.

"You weren't supposed to speak to him," she snapped as I shut the locker door and peeked at her face. I was right. She was annoyed.

"I couldn't just ignore him, Kate; that's not how I was raised." I sighed, closing my eyes and pinching the bridge of my nose with my forefinger and thumb. His sweet smell was still overpowering my senses and I was starting to get a migraine.

"Yeah, well, you know, Suranne, when it comes to—" Her voice was cut short by someone clearing their throat. "Hey babe, could you do me a favour?" The delectably smooth, deep voice rang in my ears. I stiffened and at once was engulfed in that luscious smell of Kane Richards's cologne.

"Err . . . sure," I heard Kate answer breathlessly and opened my eyes to glare at her. Here *she* was snapping at *me* when she's drooling over him just the same. Hypocritical or what? Kane raised an eyebrow at Kate whilst she stared wide-eyed at him.

"Move," he said, like the answer was stupidly obvious and this time I turned to glare at Kane. How could girls be dim-witted enough to *like* this guy? He spoke to them like they were

13

pieces of dirt. Kate just stood there dumbfounded for a second before her cheeks went red and she stared at the floor.

"Sure," she mumbled, trudging off. I could commiserate with how she felt and stared at her back retreating down the hallway. Once again I heard Kane clearing his throat. I took a deep breath and turned back to him.

*Whoa* . . .

He was standing *much* closer than I expected; his arm stretched above our heads, resting his palm on the roof of my locker, whilst his other hand was tucked in his jeans pocket. His head was slightly ducked and his thick black eyelashes were casting long shadows across his cheekbones. His lips were parted as he slowly eyed my body from the waist upwards before curving up into a smile.

"You know, that wasn't very nice. Do you have *any* respect for girls at all?"

He shrugged lightly, his eyes still moving up my body. They lingered at my neck and his smile grew wider. "Sure I do, but she was in my way so . . ." he trailed off as his eyes reached my face, slowly travelling up until they finally reached my eyes.

"What do you want?" I demanded. His presence was messing with my mind and I was beginning to become flustered, with his aroma swirling around me and his silky voice hugging my eardrums. I needed some air, and fast.

He leaned his face even closer to mine, and licked his bottom lip ever so slightly before grazing it with his teeth. "I need a favour," he murmured, his breath fanning across my face, his musical voice dominating my mind.

This wasn't going to be as easy as I'd thought.

"What could I possibly give you that no one else can?"

He chuckled and glanced down at my body again, shrugging his eyebrows rather suggestively. *"Well . . ."* he started before I interrupted him.

"If you're after sex you can forget it. I've only been here a day and I can pretty much figure out the type of guy you are," I said through clenched teeth, remembering the girl who stood next to him when he was sitting at my desk. I mean he couldn't even remember her *name!* No way was I going to be one of those girls. Kate was right. I should just ignore him.

I stood there waiting for his comeback or an egotistical comment of some kind about how I would regret it but he didn't say a word. He just continued to stare at me, his light brown eyes seeming to be calculating something.

"OK, then." He lowered his arm and strolled down the corridor. I stared after him, my mind blank. Is that it? Just "OK, then?" What does that mean? Was that really what he was after? *Sex?*

I huffed angrily and headed for the canteen to look for Kate. My eyes roamed over the various tables, but I spotted Kane first, already seated with his perfectly toned arm around some straight-haired brunette, smiling at him like she had just won the lottery. I looked around the room again and mercifully spotted Kate sitting at a table. I quickly joined her and slung my bag on the floor.

"Hey," she muttered quietly, she seemed a little glum.

"Hey," I replied back in a low voice. There was no more conversation after that. We both picked at our food silently, and I was a hundred percent sure that Kane Richards was on her mind.

He was definitely on mine.

15

If I thought the first day was bad, it only got worse. There was more than one reason for this. Firstly, my teachers were persistently giving me hell because I was constantly zoning out in their lessons, even though they realised that I already knew everything they were teaching me.

Secondly, the weather in South Carolina had turned unbearably hot. Back home, if it was sunny any time other than summer it was a blessing, and as a rule, we enjoyed it while it lasted. I had grown up with the climate there, was used to it, quite comfortable with it, even. So having this kind of weather in February was madness. I was sure I was going to become ill if it stayed this hot any longer.

And the last reason was the most annoying, and the most unbearable. It was unbearable because Kane Richards completely ignored me. It was as if I didn't exist. He didn't speak to me, didn't look at me, he didn't acknowledge my presence whatsoever. I knew that this should be a good thing; after all he was possibly the worst form of guy out there. But I couldn't help it. I kept thinking back to our last conversation and how he had so casually walked away from me.

Already my mind was agitated, wondering about what he could have possibly meant. Already I was yearning for him to be back in front of me again so I could smell him, see his smile, listen to his wondrous voice.

I was like this already. And he'd spoken to me *twice*.

Slowly I began to realise that I wasn't *going* to become one of those girls who had been dreamily sighing about him just yesterday. I wasn't *going* to be like the girls who had greeted him so eagerly upon his approach and had watched his every move with rapt interest.

Oh no. Because instead, I realised something else.

I already *was* one.

# 4. DISCOVERY

## Suzanne

"You would think that as someone who enjoys female company so much, he would be kissing her like crazy. It's obvious she's dying to make out with him."

It was a Friday, and Kate, Lawrence, and I were sitting at a table in the canteen. Across the way stood Kane Richards; his arm casually thrown round a wavy-haired blonde with a huge bust and long legs. She had her arm around his waist and was gazing at his face like she had seen the sun for the first time. I couldn't blame her. I would be staring at him like that as well.

"Kane doesn't kiss his chicks," Lawrence snorted whilst he picked at a breakfast bar with his fingers.

"*Really?*" I asked. That seemed weird; you would think that he'd at least kiss these girls before he slept with them. Surely they wouldn't just jump into bed with him without any effort on his part. But as I stared at him, I could easily believe that they did. He was wearing a clean, crisp white shirt today. The collar was stiff so it must have been brand new, and the sleeves were rolled up around his firmly toned forearms. The front of his hair was spiked up neatly as always, and he wore dark jeans with a black belt, the buckle just slightly showing over his shirt.

"Yeah, well not on the lips anyway; he's happy to kiss anywhere else," Kate said rolling her eyes. "Everyone assumes that it's some kind of statement, that the girl who he does kiss on the lips will be like 'The One.'" She raised her fingers into quotation marks as she said that and chuckled.

I had never noticed before. I was usually too busy staring at his body, or his face, but it was true. For the past three weeks, he'd never once kissed any of the girls on the lips. And it wasn't like he didn't have many to choose from. Every lunchtime meant a different girl he had his arms around, kissing her forehead gently whilst she giggled and blushed.

"He's gonna be sitting with us by the way. He told me at practice," Lawrence announced dryly, still picking at his food.

"*What*?!" Kate hissed, glaring at Lawrence. "Why didn't you tell him *No*? He never sits here!"

Lawrence just shrugged and continued picking at his food broodingly. I felt guilty watching him sitting there. I hadn't really paid much attention to him since the whole locker thing, and only now noticed that this seemed to be his usual mood recently.

"What's wrong, Lawrence?" I asked gently. He was sitting opposite me and Kate, so I got up and switched sides, sitting in the empty seat beside him and shuffled it closer to his side.

He just shrugged weakly. "'s nothin' I guess," he murmured.

Although I no longer felt any attraction towards Lawrence—mostly due to the fact that my attention was solely directed at Kane—I still found him unbelievably cute. His clear blue eyes were the most prominent feature on his face. They literally shone against his skin, and seeing them sad was discomforting. I leaned closer to him and his lower lip jutted out slightly before he groaned and leaned his head on my shoulder.

"Life's shit," he whined before sighing and closing his eyes, seemingly pleased with his new position.

"Tell me about it," Kate muttered sourly. "And thanks to *you* it's gonna get a whole lot worse."

"He would've come anyway Kate, you know that," Lawrence announced, his voice seemed brighter as his head rested on my shoulder and I stroked his hair instinctively. He reminded me of an adorable little brother you wanted to cuddle. He sighed contently and seemed to relax a little.

"Well this is *cozy*." The sound of *his* voice was like some kind of addictive drug. The fact that I hadn't heard it in almost three weeks had been giving me withdrawal symptoms and hearing it now gave me some kind of internal high as the smooth words embraced my ears once again. Lawrence sighed and sat up, whilst Kane pulled up a chair next to him. I frowned, wondering what was wrong with the empty chair next to Kate.

I realised that he didn't have the blonde tucked under his arm anymore. Kate seemed to notice too, and raised an eyebrow at him. "Where's your latest piece of meat?" she asked sarcastically, but Kane just shrugged and looked at me for the first time in what felt like forever. I tried to prevent myself from hyperventilating, and focused on taking deep breaths instead of on the light brown that dominated his eyes.

"I told her to go eat, she was boring me," he replied, still looking at me.

"Boring you? I assume you had *sex* with her last night?" Kate challenged. Kane looked at her then, and raised an eyebrow. "So?"

Making a disgusted noise in the back of her throat, Kate leaned back in her seat and folded her arms whilst Kane started talking to Lawrence about some basketball game. Only the smaller part of my mind was keeping tabs on what was happening around me. The rest of my mind was focusing on his face. A certain thought had come to me and so I stared at him as he chatted and laughed with Lawrence before the curiosity got the better of me and I had to ask.

"Why don't you kiss girls on the lips?" I blurted out, interrupting their conversation, and all three of them turned to look at me stunned. I kept my eyes on him.

He shrugged casually. "I have no desire to. If I wanted to, I would."

I cocked my head to the side whilst my mind processed his answer. So he had the desire to sleep with these girls, but not kiss them? Kane must have assumed that I wasn't going to comment on his answer, considering that he turned back to Lawrence and continued his conversation.

"You know, some people seem to think it's a statement," I blurted out again, and like before, all of them turned to stare at me. Kate looked angry, like I was saying something I shouldn't. Kane looked curious and Lawrence slightly frustrated.

"A statement of what?"

"People think that it's some kind of imperceptible certainty that the girl you *do* kiss on the lips will inevitably be 'The One.'" I shaped my fingers into quotation marks like Kate had done earlier. Both of them turned back to Kane awaiting his reaction as I stared at him with nothing but curiosity in my eyes.

"What do you think?" he asked, arching a perfect thick brow.

I shrugged before voicing my opinion.

"I think it's a subconscious attempt to make yourself feel better. It's believed that kissing on the lips is a higher assertion of intimacy than sex itself, and that maybe if you *don't* kiss them, you won't feel so guilty about *jerking* them around. Of course, if this *is* true, then it means that there is hope for you after all," I announced nonchalantly, even though my heart was racing in my chest. "Maybe you're not a complete arsehole in spite of everything else."

My outburst seemed to take everyone by surprise. Kane had his eyebrows raised, but there was a slight tension in his jaw which convinced me that I was right. Lawrence once again looked frustrated and Kate just stared at me in awe, before eyeing Kane up and down to consider whether my opinion was even possible.

Kane chuckled somewhat tightly, as if forcing out the sound and then playfully punched Lawrence on the shoulder. "Dude, I gotta go, coach said he wanted to speak to me 'bout somethin'. Catch you later." After that, he stood up and walked off without another word.

I smirked whilst staring at his retreating figure. It seemed I had touched a nerve.

Maybe cracking Kane Richards wasn't going to be difficult after all.

# 5. IMPRESSED

## Kane

I sat on the bed with my back against the headboard as this brunette was straddling me and nibbling on my neck. The strong beat of some Xzibit song resounded through her stereo, vibrating through the foundation of the house. The heavy bass rang through my ears as she unbuttoned my shirt, and her breathing became heavier.

The words coming from the stereo surrounded me as her hands reached my belt buckle. I closed my eyes waiting for the real action to start, and instantly behind my lids, was Suranne smiling as she sat at the table with Lawrence on her shoulder.

Suddenly I felt some unfamiliar emotion flow through my veins and pushed the brunette off and sat up. Why the *hell* was I so angry all of a sudden? And why was she even on my mind when I had a hot chick all over me? I felt my fists clench and my body stiffen as the image of Suranne stroking Lawrence's hair flashed in my mind.

"What's wrong, baby?" The brunette purred in my ear seductively and took my ear lobe in her mouth, nibbling on it slightly. OK, I usually loved this shit. I should have been turned on already, eager to get the evening started.

This can not be happening to me, I thought, as I glanced down and willed my *man* to come back to life and work his wonders, keeping up the Kane Richards name. But nothing happened. Nothing. Not even a *twitch*.

The brunette was peppering kisses down my chest now and her hands were slowly sliding down my abs. *Christ.*

Pushing her off again I started to rub my temples with my fingers, squeezing my eyes shut, but instantly regretted it when her face flashed behind my eyelids; her deep mahogany hair and profound gray eyes staring back at me widely. I began to get a headache and the brunette started rubbing her hands all over my shoulders and down my chest again.

"Turn this crap off will you? I'm getting a headache," I muttered, shrugging out from under her grip. All of a sudden the thought of this girl all over me turned my stomach and I decided to get the hell up out of there and maybe get some fresh air. Sighing heavily, I heaved myself off the bed, doing the buttons back up on my shirt.

"Oh, *come on.* Don't leave already," she whined, her lips slipping into a pout. "We haven't even got to the best bit yet." She smirked and winked at me suggestively, but it still did nothing for me. I growled inside my head, begging to get some response down below.

Nope. Nothing.

No way was I going to become impotent just because some new chick with a hot accent and a slamming body decides she wants to put up a fight. I'm *Kane Richards* for Christ's sake. They all cave in the end, just seems like she might take longer than I thought.

"Earth *to Kaaaannnee*?!" the brunette wailed, waving her hand in front of me and pulling me from my thoughts. I sighed and carried on fastening the buttons on my shirt. "Look . . ." I glanced at her, raising my eyebrows waiting for her to say her name.

"Rachel," she growled, glaring at me.

"Look, Rachel, maybe another time, babe." I replied, focusing on a text that I just received on my cell. It was one of my boys letting me know about some new joint in town, and asking whether I'll be there hitting it up. A party ain't shit without me and everyone knows it. I tapped in my reply and made my way out the door of this 'Rachel's' place and into my ride.

"Why don't you kiss girls on the lips?" she had asked. I smiled at the memory of her voice as she was stating her own theory as to why I didn't kiss them. I had been considering her words, wondering if there was any truth to them. It was true that I felt it was a bit too . . . intimate. But it was more about the fact that I just never *wanted* to. I never felt the desire pulling at me to kiss them. Maybe she was right then? Maybe I *was* trying to make myself feel better? I knew there was some truth in her words, but she could go to hell if she thought I was planning to admit that to her. No one knew about my life, my preferences, and no one cared. And that was exactly how I wanted to keep it.

For the rest of the night she stayed on my mind; her words constantly nagging at my conscience, the image of her defiant face and raised brow stitched firmly behind my eye sockets. This girl was going to be a challenge for me, there was no doubt about that. But I was damn certain that it was going to be a challenge I would enjoy. One that would definitely keep me entertained throughout the school day.

Chuckling lightly to myself, I turned on the radio, turning the volume dial as high as it would go, as I headed towards the city. A smirk pulled at my lips as the air whipped in through the windows and I began to pick up speed.

*Suranne Williams.*

I wanted her.

And Kane Richards *always* got what he wanted.

# 6. SURPRISE

## Suranne

"Hey you two, I'll meet you at the car, yeah?" I said to Kate and Lawrence. It was a Saturday, and Kate had asked me to go into town with them just for something to do. For the past three hours we had been going from shop to shop looking at clothes. Something Lawrence was obviously bored by, until I decided to start looking for him. We shoved him into various garments, taking pictures as he wandered over to the fancy dress section and pranced about dressed as a pirate. When he dressed up as James Bond, even I had to appreciate his looks. He really did look quite nice in black.

But now I was exhausted, and the weather was once again unbearably hot. Kate and Lawrence wanted to go on to different stores but I couldn't take the heat for much longer, and noticed a small park that had a bench perched right under a huge maple tree. Perfect shade.

"You sure? You don't look so good." Kate's eyes roamed over my face and she cocked an eyebrow.

"No, no, I'll be fine. It's just the heat, honestly. Umm, I'll meet you at the car in like an hour or so," I reassured her. If I didn't get out of this heat soon I was going to pass out.

Both Kate and Lawrence shrugged before strolling back towards the shops, whilst I wandered over to the bench. The bench overlooked a small pond that reflected the blue sky and buildings beautifully. Random joggers passed now and then with their earphones plugged in, and a light breeze was blowing.

The shade from the tree gave me instant relief, and I sighed happily as I sank down onto the bench. It was so peaceful there, and I decided to listen to some calming music. I knew that if I didn't distract myself, my thoughts would automatically wander to *him*. I didn't want to say his name, the same name that was probably on a hundred girls' minds, whilst he sat around and bragged about his latest triumph of getting into another girl's pants. I pulled out my iPod and swirled my thumb over the touch navigator swiftly searching for the song that would fit the scenery. I didn't know why, but classical struck me as perfect for the scenery, and so I put on my favourite piano composition by Yiruma.

As the music trilled in my ears, I began to relax even more and closed my eyes in contentment. I imagined myself playing the song on a beautiful grand piano, my fingers flowing freely over the ivory keys. Not many people knew about my love for playing, apart from my mum. It was my own personal way of expressing who I was and how I felt. I was never good with words and could never open up to anyone. Not even my mother. Playing was my best outlet.

My fingers automatically waved in the air as I pictured the notes I would be pressing. I hummed along as the song reached the bridge and smiled to myself before suddenly feeling pressure on the bench next to me. I gasped, snapped open my eyes, and jumped to my feet.

Sitting there on the bench a foot away from me in all of his glorious beauty, was none other than Kane Richards.

# 7. FIRST THOUGHTS

## Kane

I continued smirking at her, trying to hide my suddenly sweaty palms and accelerated heart rate. *Well, that's never happened before. What the hell was wrong with me?*

"What the *hell* are you doing here?" Suranne breathed and folded her arms across her chest, glaring at me.

The angry tone of her voice, coupled with her accent and the slanted pout of her lips caused a familiar tingle in my lower abdomen, and I found myself clearing my throat while I discretely readjusted myself.

"I was driving home when I noticed Lawrence's car. I thought I could catch up with him. Didn't expect to see you here though," I added sourly, and cocked an eyebrow questioningly.

She shrugged in response, "He and Kate asked me to come out with them; I was too hot though, and told them to go on without me." She frowned at something and then sighed, relaxing back on the bench. The closeness of her body screamed at me, I was tempted to pull her to me; the fact that I was uncontrollably hard for the first time in two days didn't help.

I looked at her face; her eyes were closed as a breeze blew past us, and she bit on the bottom of her lip softly. I stifled a groan as her actions caused more stirring down below. I wanted to be the one biting down on that lip, pulling her close to me.

*But I didn't kiss chicks, though? Right.*

31

"So," I cleared my throat again and grinned at her crookedly, "what was with the floating fingers, huh? Is there some invisible instrument you're not telling me about?" I chuckled and raised an eyebrow. Her eyes widened and her face flushed a delicate pink before she ducked her head and looked down at the ground. I had to admit she was even cuter when she blushed.

"I was, umm, listening to a piano tune, and imagining playing it . . . that's all," she mumbled softly before returning my gaze, looking rather sheepish.

Huh. So she's in to classical music? And she plays? That's a first.

"What song was it?" I asked softly, not wanting to embarrass her again.

"Uhh, it's uh, called "River Flows in You" by–"

"Yiruma." I finished her sentence and looked at her. I didn't know whether I was shocked or impressed. A bit of both, I think. She actually had something in *common* with me, I thought to myself. My mom never said anything when I requested to have a piano in my room; she always thought it was just for show and didn't realize that I actually enjoyed playing. I never told anyone about it, and just shrugged it off whenever anyone asked. I didn't know why but for some reason it never felt like something that needed to be shared, it almost seemed private in a way.

She gasped silently before looking at me, her gray eyes revealing nothing but curiosity.

"How do you know?" she asked. I got the feeling she didn't quite believe someone like me could possibly have interest in his kind of music. I just rolled my eyes at her assumption.

"It's one of my favorites." I shrugged and then smirked as a new thought came to me. "Can you play it?" I challenged.

She lifted her head defensively. "Yes," she said firmly before raising an eyebrow. "Can you?"

My eyes lidded slightly as her sexy voice hugged my ears, and her scent of some kind of flower or fruit enveloped me. I groaned internally and instinctively leaned closer, until my face was just an inch away from her. I heard her sharp intake of breath, and she bit down on her lip again. *Dear God,* I thought to myself. For the first time in three years, I felt that desire, an uncontrollable urge to kiss her lips.

"Yes," I whispered.

I couldn't control it anymore. I slid even closer to her on the bench, and slowly leaned my face down towards hers.

I knew that this could possibly look bad for me; knew that this could jeapordize my reputation.

Did I care?

*Hell no.*

# 8. CONFUSION

## Suranne

His lips were just centimeters away from mine. He couldn't be serious. Kane Richards *kissing* me? *Was* he serious? Did he really just want to kiss me because he had the *urge* to? Or was it just a test like the first time we had met? I didn't really want to find out.

"Show me," I whispered, causing him to stop in his tracks and pull back slightly, his expression confused.

"Show you what?" he asked, his breath fanning over my lips, his gentle voice husky and seductive. I could smell the faint hint of mint on his breath, and my body fought to repress a shudder.

"Show me you can play it," I replied simply, trying to keep myself under control. The park had become unnaturally quiet and there was no one around but him and me. No one would know if I did anything with him would they? Maybe just one kiss, maybe I should just let him, and run my fingers through his amazing hair, and possibly even tug on it a little.

*No, Suranne. Remember who this is.*

He frowned for a moment before regaining his smirk and taking my hand. My eyes immediately snapped to where our skin was connected, and I felt a light warmth travel up my arm just from his touch.

"Fine, I have a piano at my place. I have to say I didn't think you'd be that easy to get into my bedroom." He grinned and raised his eyebrows suggestively.

35

And just like that, the warm feeling vanished. I snatched my hand away from his, ignoring how I immediately missed the contact, and pushed the thought into the back of my mind.

"I'm not going to your bloody house! I don't wanna see you play *that* bad." I huffed and folded my arms, only earning a suggestive stare at my chest from Kane. I cleared my throat angrily trying to get his attention back to my face. He sighed and leaned back against the bench. "You should be honored, babe. You'd be the first girl I brought back to my room." He winked at me, before smirking once again.

What was that supposed to mean? How could he be some sex-crazed monster but not have any girls in his room?

*It's obvious he goes back to their place to do the deed. Of course.*

So then, what did that make me? My heart swelled at the idea of him actually wanting to bring me back to his house, at the possibility of me being the first. I stared back at him, unable to say anything, and felt so close to accepting his offer. I watched his jaw unclench and his face become soft. He took my hand again and leaned into me slowly.

"Look, Suranne, I – I mean, I don't . . . just think. *Damn.*" He frustratedly ran his other hand through his hair before continuing.

"You're not like *them* . . . you're not even close," he whispered.

Oh my God. I'm not even close? Did that mean that I was worse than all those other slags he had sex with, so bad that I wasn't even worth it? No wonder he didn't mind taking me back to his house, he had no desire to do anything with me. Oh, God. He didn't want to do me. My breathing became heavier and I was nearing a full-blown panic attack. Was he basically trying to say that I was unwanted?

All of a sudden anger washed through me. How dare he even come up to me, take my hand in his, lean his face in like he was about to kiss me and then tell me I was "not even close." I knew he was a pompous arse, but geez.

*How dare he?*

"What the hell is that supposed to mean?" I attempted to keep a calm and cool composure, but I was struggling greatly. I could almost see a haze cloud my vision. My muscles tightened, my mind filled with anger, my fists clenched with rage.

And my mouth burned with spitting, venomous fury.

And it was all because of Kane Richards.

I was too angry and confused to notice the somewhat bewildered expression on his face.

"What did I say?" he asked, eyes wide.

"Don't screw with me Kane, I may have been a bit forward the other day at lunch but Jesus, you didn't have to go to so much trouble to insult me. Those girls that you bang are slags and you have the nerve to say that I'm not even like them but WORSE?!" Tears started to form at the corners of my eyes.

# 9. ACHE

## Kane

She really was hot when she was angry but what the hell was she talking about?

Before I could even correct her she was gone, stomping off toward the east without hesitation, leaving me there on the bench.

Confused, and turned on as hell, I sat there just staring at the direction Suranne had headed. She was long gone by now, but I couldn't move my eyes. I couldn't move at all. My body just sat frozen while my mind furiously tried to decipher the meanings behind her outburst.

I never said she was worse than those girls. I never would. Surely she knows that. Jesus, I go to *kiss* this girl, something she knows I don't do, and she throws it back in my face. I go to take her hand and she rips it away from me. I, for the first time since God knows when, force myself to relax, and be honest with her and she screams at me.

*No shit, Kane, get the hint already.* Anyone else and I would have been done with them already. Since when has Kane-every-chick-begs-for-Richards had to chase anyone? I . . . well . . . I never have. So why should I start now?

I forced myself to move and get my ass back home when it started to get dark. I was done with the God-why-do-I-like-her-so-much shit swirling my mind. I needed my black silk sheets, I needed my TV, and I needed a drink.

Of course getting her out of my head was going to be easier said than done. God truly does hate me and will enjoy my suffering as much as possible.

By 9 p.m. I was certain that she was just dying to bang me and was denying her insufferable need by trying to act like a total bitch around me but a complete angel to everyone else. Especially Lawrence. Yeah, that's what it is. She wants me too much but doesn't want to be chucked the next day.

Cause I would chuck her the next day.

*Wouldn't I?*

Yes. She would be boring.

*Would she? Given the chance, could I have talked to her for hours?*

Damn.

By 10 p.m. I was certain that she was just in a mood and that her sexy-ass body was suffering from unavoidable PMS girly shit. That would have to be the reason why she would storm off on me. No chick ever storms off on me. I mean, *Jesus* I'm too good to look at for that shit.

But then I remembered the expression on her face before she had left. The slight shimmering of her gray eyes.

But I'd seen girls cry before. Usually when I told them to remove their skanky hands from my shirt, or my hair, or wherever they felt the need to grope me the day after. But it wasn't . . . painful for me to watch them cry. I would merely shrug and move on, telling them to do the same. I mean keeping me to one girl would just be selfish, right? I was taught to share. I was doing a good deed.

Share . . . Suddenly the thought of me having to share Suranne with anyone made my fists clench and my teeth snap.

Even though she wasn't mine to begin with. But I could change that.

Couldn't I?

I'd never felt this shit before. Images of hugging her and running my fingers through that sexy hair of hers and listening to her sexy voice filled my head. And I liked it.

What was wrong with me?

By 11 p.m. I was procrastinating sleep. I knew that if I closed my eyes she would be there. Not that it made much of a difference. She was in my head already, eyes open or closed. But I didn't want to hand myself over to my dreams. Those too real dreams where I would be with her, and she would be smiling and her hair would be flowing and her smell would be all around me. Only to wake up to an empty room knowing that wasn't the case.

I'm not that masochistic.

Shit.

By 1 a.m. I was done with all my delusional theories on what her problem was and was constantly asking myself why I even cared. She was no one. Just some girl. Who had sexy lips, and nice eyes, and a perky chest, and a firm ass that swayed when she walked and I could just imagine running my fingers down her waist and . . .

Shit.

I stared unseeingly at the moving objects on the TV screen. Nothing made sense, and I had no idea what I was watching. I glanced at my cell to check the time.

1:30 a.m.

I wondered what she was doing, whether she was up and restless because of me, like I was because of her. Would she be sleeping soundly and having dreams that didn't make her ache for them to be real when she woke up?

I looked over at the east wall of my room and stared at the object in the corner. It had been weeks, months even. For some reason I had lost the desire to walk over there and lose myself. But now it was calling to me. It sat silently against the dark corner, beckoning me to its sleek, smooth structure.

I pulled myself off my bed and padded across the room, not caring about the time, or the fact that my family was sleeping. I did the one thing that I had been refusing to do for too long.

At 1:35 a.m. I pulled out the padded black leather bench, pushed back the smooth wooden lid, and drowned myself in the ivory keys of my piano.

I let the melody run through my mind and pour out through my fingers onto the keys. Giving it a test run, I changed chords and added a random melody. I thought about how much I had this urge to be with her, see her smile, see her laugh, see her eyes close peacefully like she did when she was on the bench alone. Before I showed up and ruined it all.

I changed the tone of the melody as I thought about how she laughed and smiled when she was in school.

*I* wanted to be the reason she smiled. *I* wanted to be the reason she laughed. Dammit, *I* wanted to be the reason she was peaceful. Instead I made her angry.

I brought the melody to an end, shifting it to a lower, melancholy key, and slumped on the bench. The urge. The *ache* to be with her was pulsing strongly and I didn't feel calmer, as I'd hoped. I felt worse.

I went back over to my bed and picked up my cell glancing at the time again.

1:50 a.m.

*If I can't sleep because of her than why the hell should she?*

I put on some pants and a black tee and grabbed my car keys.

The melody of my piano playing still strolled through my mind. I had to see her. Whether she wanted me to or not.

# 10. WORDLESS COMMUNICATION

## Suranne

I huffed, threw the covers off my body and glanced at the time on my phone.

2 a.m.

Groaning, I laid flat on my back, listening to the faint tick of the huge clock my aunt had downstairs. Staring at the ceiling I tried to lose myself in the noise of the constant ticking, hoping that I could be lulled into sleep. I took a deep breath and just listened.

*Tick, tick, tick, tick, tick*

Keeping my eyes fastened on the ceiling I tried to blink less often, and felt my eyelids getting heavier.

*Tick, tick, tick, tick, tick*

I blinked even slower now, and each time I did, my eyes stayed closed much longer than the last.

*Tick, tick, tick, tick*

*"Psst!"*

I frowned but kept my eyes closed, staying with the rhythm of the clock and trying to ignore any other sounds, like some animal outside my window.

*Tick, tick, tick, tick*

*"PSSST!!"* The noise was louder, and for some strange reason, didn't entirely resemble an animal.

"Suranne! Wake up!" it hissed.

I bolted upright out of bed and glanced at the night sky through my window. Oh, God. I recognised that voice. It couldn't be.

Could it?

I slowly slid my legs to the edge of the bed, and pulled myself upright, taking small, wobbly steps to the window. I glanced downwards, then gasped and clutched my chest with my hand, trying to lower my heartbeat.

There, on the front drive of my aunt's house, was Kane Richards, using his phone as a light, peering at the front of the house and hissing my name.

I took a deep breath and started chanting to myself to keep calm.

*Don't be happy he's here. Don't be happy he's here.*

*Oh my God he's here! Why is he here?!*

*Calm down, Suranne. Breathe.*

I peeked at his figure once again, and smiled. He obviously didn't notice me standing here watching him, and I could faintly hear him mumbling to himself.

"Shit! . . . getting myself into . . . probably hit me . . . face is too good for that."

I rolled my eyes and lifted up my window.

"What do you want, Kane?" I sighed as his head snapped up, and his glorious lips turned up in a faint smile.

"Suranne," he breathed; his voice almost sounded relieved to see me, but I guessed it was more from not having to hiss my name like an idiot at two in the morning than from seeing my face.

I sighed inwardly. If only.

"Well, duh," I tried to put on my best American accent and rolled my eyes at him. "Who else would it be?"

He laughed and looked down at the grass before fidgeting with his phone.

Hmm . . . Kane Richards looked uncomfortable . . . almost nervous. Well this should be interesting.

"How do you even know where I live?" I asked in a low voice, hoping not to wake my aunt.

He shrugged.

"I googled your aunt. Found the address pretty easy." His head snapped up at me and his lips curved into a small smile "Hey, could you come down? I need to talk to you."

"Hold on a sec," I replied and pulled my window shut, turned, and quietly did a little victory dance, before pulling myself together.

"Be angry, he insulted you," I murmured to myself, but couldn't control the grin that was plastered on my face.

I looked for some suitable shoes, but all I could see were my fluffy bunny slippers, and I could just imagine his face when he spotted them. I don't think I could deal with Kane Richards making a laughing stock out of me at this time of morning.

*Christ.*

Where were my flats? I couldn't exactly go out there in heels, that would be ridiculous, but those damn slippers were definitely out of the question.

I'd just have to go barefoot.

I tried smoothing my hair out of its animalistic state and slowly crept down the stairs to the front door. I opened it quietly and stepped out onto the front porch, folding my arms in the process.

Kane was standing further down the drive, with his perfectly toned back to me, and his hand was running through his hair. His tight black top showed his muscles flexing from the movement perfectly, and I bit my lip as my eyes raked over his luscious frame.

"Well?" I asked, with one eyebrow raised. He spun around, and his eyes widened as he slowly stared at my body. I'd forgotten that I was only wearing boy shorts and a tank top and mentally screamed at myself for forgetting to put on some trousers. His eyes continued to run up my legs and rested on my hips before I smirked and cleared my throat.

"If you've woken me up at two in the bloody morning only to ogle at my legs you can piss off," I muttered, and his head snapped up to my eyes, before his face softened and he smiled warmly at me.

God, his smile was sexy.

I put my hands on my hips and waited for him to talk, but he just ran his hand through his hair again and continued blinking at me. I could tell he was thinking about something, but I really didn't want to stand there forever.

I deliberately sighed and folded my arms again, waiting for him to start, but decided that I was going to start for him. I glared at his face before I spoke.

"You know, you could begin with an apology," I announced firmly, but his face went dark and his eyes seemed to focus again.

"Suranne," he breathed quietly, "I don't know what I said." His voice seemed strained, and his eyes were shining at me, burning into me whilst his expression looked pleading.

I took a deep breath, as I felt the saliva in my mouth turn sour at the memory of his words.

"You said I wasn't even close to those other girls, which means that I'm worse right? I mean jeez, if those girls are skanks and you think I'm worse?" I breathed a laugh and shook my head in disbelief.

I felt the stinging in my eyes as his words rang through me again. Why did it hurt so much? I tried to swallow my tears and the lump in my throat. I really didn't want to cry in front of this guy.

Even in the darkness I could see his eyes flash.

"Is that what you think?!" he almost growled and took two long strides over to me and pushed me up against the front door, leaving me breathless, staring into his face. His eyes seemed to be conveying something I couldn't quite distinguish. Almost anger, but I wasn't sure.

"It's what you said," I whispered in reply.

He closed his eyes, clenched his jaw, and leaned his forehead against mine.

"I was trying to say that you're better than them. That you're different in a good way," he breathed, so quietly that I had to push my face closer just to hear him, but this action also caused me to be within a millimetre of his mouth. I could feel his hot breath against my face, and I stared at his perfect red lips, so close to mine, then peeked up at his eyes, only to find them open and watching me.

He slowly slid his hands up my arms, making me shiver, and cupped my face firmly.

"I don't give a shit that you're a total bitch to me, I don't give a shit that it's like three in the morning, and I certainly don't give a shit if this isn't what you want," he growled, took one last look at my mouth and then roughly pressed his lips against mine. They were warm, and firm as I melted into his embrace, moving my lips with his. He groaned into my mouth and licked my bottom lip, and I granted him entrance, parting my lips slowly as our lips moved gently against each other.

"Suranne! Honey, is that you?" Aunt Clacy called from behind the front door and Kane pulled away abruptly, both of us gasping for air.

"Christ," I breathed, my mind going into a silent frenzy at the feel of Kane's lips against mine.

"Umm, yeah . . . i—it's me, just give me a minute," I stammered weakly, as Kane pulled back a step with a grin on his face.

He winked at me and chuckled before coming closer and kissing my forehead.

"I'll see you tomorrow," he murmured gently, before walking back to his car, pulling out of the driveway and disappearing all together.

I walked back inside, and waved off my aunt's questioning glare, my smile growing wider with every step I took toward my bedroom.

I smiled to myself and shook my head as I sat down on the edge of my bed.

Some talk that was.

# 11. Background Truths

## Kane

As I made my way up my porch steps I still had a huge grin on my face. My mind was still going over that kiss, and those damn lips. I chuckled and shook my head minutely as I thought about the kinda pull my girl had over me.

I stood still in my tracks and gaped at myself.

*My girl?*

My mind never thought shit like that, but I wasn't denying the fact that it sounded damn good to me.

I continued shaking my head but put it down to the sleep deprivation. It was after three in the morning after all. I just needed some sleep.

I put my keys quietly in the door and tiptoed in silently, trying not to wake Mom. The last thing I needed was that. But like I said before, God truly does hate me, and with that, the lights snapped on and standing there in her nightgown looking dirty, drunk, and depressed she stood.

Dammit.

"Where the hell have you been?" she slurred. I bit back a grimace at her appearance. Fair enough if she wanted to make herself feel like crap. Hell, even if she tried dragging *me* down with her. But my sister didn't deserve this. She was twelve for Christ's sake.

I clenched my jaw as I stared at her bloodshot puffy eyes and matted brown hair. A half empty glass of some clear liquid was shaking in her hand. She looked like hell. But telling her so would get us nowhere and I really didn't have the energy for it. So I sighed, and walked up to her, took her arm carefully, and led her to the stairs.

"Nowhere, Mom. It's late. You should get some rest," I murmured softly, pleading with my eyes to *please* just this once not make a scene.

*Please, don't let her make a scene . . .*

But I was startled out of my silent chanting when I heard the familiar sound of glass coming into contact with and shattering against the kitchen floor as my mom yanked her arm away from me with vigor.

"Don't give me that *shit*! . . . I'm your mother, you will *answer me!*" she spat, swaying towards the kitchen counter unsteadily. Her eyes danced crazily from her inebriated state, but flashed with anger when I reflexively reached out to steady her.

"Mom, you need to get a grip, this shit ain't fair to Ashley," I sighed, running a hand through my hair and holding the roots tightly. I really was too tired for this, and I'd be swaying myself if I didn't get to sleep.

She slapped my hand away and gripped the counter to keep herself upright. "You think I don't *know* that!" she hissed at me, her words coming out in a slurred, but vicious tone. "You think I don't think about that everyday? You think I don't see the pity in your eyes every time you *look* at me?" She glared at me and let out a slow humorless chuckle, then her face twisted slightly as she gazed down at the floor where the shards of glass and alcohol were scattered. She grimaced, and I realized when I spotted the empty bottle on the counter, that she wasn't grimacing at the mess she'd made, but at the fact that she'd wasted her last bit of alcohol.

My teeth clamped shut with an audible snap, and I pushed past her to get the brush and dustpan from the cupboard to clean up. She continued gazing absently as I cleaned up all the pieces of glass.

"Your father would be proud," she whispered, still staring blankly at the floor, her eyes glazed over.

I felt the anger boil up in me, and stiffened. My fists clenched tightly against the brush handle. My skin stretched painfully over my knuckles as I tried to take calming breaths but all I could hear were her words and her raspy breaths surrounding me. She had no *right* to even mention him when she stood there drunk and wallowing. She knew it.

I snapped my head up at her, and glowered at her face, realizing that I just didn't have it in me anymore to deal with it. With her. I never thought that I could lose respect for the woman who brought me into this world, but she proved me wrong. *Way to go.*

"Fuck you," I spat back at her, rising off the floor and emptying the glass in the trash before stomping past her, not caring if she made it to her room or not. She could fall down the stairs if she wanted to. I just didn't care.

But as I pushed my door open and slammed it behind me, I turned around to find Ashley nervously fidgeting on my bed, and knew this wasn't just about me. My lamp cast a small glow on her freckled face and short black ponytail as she frowned down at her fingers on her lap.

Even if I wanted to push my mother out of my life and just break free from all the hassle she caused me every time I came home, I couldn't.

I couldn't leave my little sister to deal with the shit that I've had to. And therefore I couldn't give up. I sighed and made my way over to the bed and plopped down next to her.

"Hey, dipshit," I murmured, nudging her shoulder with mine playfully. She glanced up at me and gave me a wide smile, her freckled cheeks pushing up into her brown eyes and the dimple in her chin making an appearance.

All of the crap she had to witness and she was still capable of having that wide-ass smile.

I chuckled at her and shook my head, mussing her hair until she whined and slapped my hands away half-heartedly.

She sighed, and her lower lip jutted out slightly as she dropped her head and stared at the floor.

"Mom's drinking again," she whispered silently into the air, her words hanging in the atmosphere.

I sighed again and put my head in my hands, frustrated and thoroughly exhausted.

"Yeah, I know," I groaned into my hands, as my fingers tugged on my hair lightly. "Don't worry kid, I'll fix it, 'K?" I reassured her, lifting my head up to meet her gaze and forcing a smile on my face. Her forehead creased; I could see the tears welling up in her eyes and it killed me to know that she was hurting and I couldn't do anything about it. Which only made me more angry at the woman downstairs. I knew there was no way for me to fix it.

And deep down, Ashley knew it too.

I nudged her off my bed and mussed her hair up again, chuckling at her protests.

"Kaaanne . . ." she whined, trying to free herself. I snickered at her weak protest and dropped my hand from her hair.

"Go to sleep. It's late." I rolled my eyes at her as she flipped me the finger and giggled, dodging the pillow I threw at her, before giving me a small wave and heading out the door.

Feeling tired, powerless, frustrated and just . . . defeated, I groaned, turned off the lamp and slid under the covers of my bed. I didn't even bother to get undressed, wanting just to forget and lose myself to those dreams.

Those dreams of her. Her gray eyes. Her voice.

I smiled to myself lazily as I let the memories of her lips against mine lull me into what I hoped finally would be a peaceful sleep.

Waking up to find my mother sprawled on the kitchen floor, her mouth open and drooling, snoring lightly, frustrated me to no end. I tried to get Ashley out the front door, but she insisted on getting some breakfast.

There was nothing I could do.

So now, I'm driving with Ashley sitting next to me, silent tears sliding down her small freckled cheeks, and quiet sniffles filling the space between us.

I was way too tired for this.

My fists clenched the wheel and I sighed. "Ashley, I didn't want you to see Mom like that," I murmured gently, handing her another Kleenex from the glove compartment. She snorted and took the tissue from me softly.

"What does it matter, she's usually worse when you're not around anyway," she replied dryly.

I winced, now feeling guilty for not being around all the time. But I needed a break, too, right? And then I realized that Ashley couldn't do that. How did she ever get a break? She definitely deserved one, and yet I still went out every night, getting laid as a distraction. Ashley pulled me out of my thoughts once we reached her school.

"So, umm, I guess you'll be out again tonight, huh?" she asked softly, staring at her hands in her lap.

"*Damn,*" I whispered to myself, realizing that I needed to sort this stuff in my life out before I could make it better. And that meant that for now, Ashley and Mom had to be my main priority. Here I was messing around, trying to push away all the shit left behind after my dad died, but it was no use. It was starting to affect my baby sister, more than it should.

I had to take time out.

Time out from the drinking. Time out from the parties. Time out from the chicks.

But the worst of it all is that I had to take time out from *her.*

My girl, with her damn gray orbs, and those full red lips. Her sexy ass and her accent, and her smell that got me rock hard. I had to let it go for now. I couldn't play around anymore.

I don't know why but my chest tightened at the thought and I felt myself becoming heavily depressed already. I heaved a deep sigh and pinched the bridge of my nose willing myself to calm down before speaking.

"Don't worry Ash, I'll be there, OK?" I murmured, snapping my eyes shut, reluctant to say those words.

*You have to do it*, I chanted over and over in my mind, before slowly opening my eyes and looking over at Ashley. She was sporting that full grin, her eyes crinkling at the side and her full, freckled cheeks pushed up.

"Really? You're really gonna be at home today?" she asked, her eyes shining.

I understood then that even though this sacrifice was gonna kill me, I'd do anything to see that smile, so I returned the grin, mussed her hair, and nodded my head firmly.

"Sure kid. Now get to school, before I kick your ass," I chuckled. She scowled at me and stuck out her tongue before bouncing out of the car toward the school building.

I was regretting my words already; my head was at a firm bridge of indecision that I really didn't want to cross.

And I hadn't even caught sight of Suranne yet.

God knows how hard it would be when I actually spotted her. Maybe I should just go back home and force Mom to sort herself out, and hope she would listen and everything would be fixed in a day.

I laughed darkly, shaking my head at my delusional thoughts.

Mythical creatures would be walking around the world before that ever happened.

I let out a breath that I hadn't even realized I'd been holding and revved the engine, pulling out of the parking lot toward my own school.

Where she would be.

I smiled, and sighed longingly as I thought again of when I'd kissed her. The urge to act on that impulse was still a mystery to me. I didn't even feel that way three years ago when the girl I thought I had lo—

No.

Not going there.

I still couldn't get my mind around the pull she had on me, and I knew kissing her felt right.

Too right.

I groaned at what I would have to do to make sure she wasn't a distraction anymore. My whole being was reluctant to do it. Mind, body, and soul were screaming in protest as I pulled into the lot. My mind was desperately trying to find a way around this. As my brain incessantly rummaged through various strategies, a certain train of thought emerged.

Why couldn't I just explain it to her?

Tell her to give me some time, just wait for me while I got a grip on the tightrope that was my shitty life.

But how would I say it?

"Listen I think you're really hot, and your lips felt heavenly, but right now my Mom's a heavily depressed drunk and my sister's an emotional twelve-year-old who depends on me to make everything better, but I have no idea how to do it, and so I have to figure this shit out before I can think of anyone else." I snorted to myself; she'd think I was an emotional dick, then I'd definitely lose her. I hadn't even considered what she'd be like when I saw her. What if she went around screaming down the halls that I kissed her? It didn't really bother me; for some unfathomable reason I would feel almost proud that she'd wanna flaunt that shit.

It would just make it worse for her after I pretty much blew her off. It would just make her confused, and she'd probably cut my balls off or whatever she does when she's angry, and I really wouldn't be able to deal with it this morning. I was equally confused.

I had never felt this way before. All I could think about were those warm lips, and the feel of her silky skin under my touch, and what it would feel like to have her underneath me, me pressing against her body, and her moaning in my ear as I grazed my teeth against her neck, and her raspy groans in my ear as I wrapped her thigh around me and . . . damn!

The last thing I needed was to be sporting a raging hard-on in the middle of school. I had two hours to sort things out before I saw her again.

# 12. CRUSHED EXPECTATIONS

## Suzanne

To say that I was a wreck Monday morning would be an understatement. I had no idea what to expect at all.

I didn't know whether to even acknowledge Kane that morning. Would I speak to him, or would he speak to me? Would I smile, just to let him know that I wasn't ignoring him? What if he just acted as if nothing had happened?

I couldn't deal with the nerves fluttering in the pit of my stomach; I had no idea what to do.

And I didn't have a clue what I would do if he ignored what happened last night, especially when I knew I wouldn't be able to. Last night as I lay down on my bed, different questions swirled in my mind. Was it just a test for him to see if he could kiss future female targets after I confronted him about it Friday?

Was I just some human lab rat for his experiments? But if that were the case why didn't he test it on anyone else? Hell, there were definitely enough girls for it.

As I walked down the halls, I spotted Lawrence and Kate speaking by my locker, and I approached them catching their current conversation.

". . . yeah, so my dad says I gotta buy these damn flowers for my mom to prove that I quote "appreciate" her and crap." Kate snickered, rolling her eyes before turning to me and smiling warmly.

"Wow, that sucks. But you should totally buy carnations, they're subtly elegant and majestic. Even though some people think they lack class, they're actually an exceptionally beautiful flower." Lawrence spoke nonchalantly, with a shrug of the shoulder and a smirk on his face whilst Kate and I just gaped at him. Both in worry and in awe. We continued staring at him for a few seconds, frozen by his words.

"Lawrence . . ." Kate breathed, "you have never sounded so much like a girl than just now." She choked, her jaw slack and her eyes wide, eyeing him worriedly. I could feel the laughter bubbling up in me, but hurting Lawrence's feelings wasn't something I wanted to do. However, that was *before* he'd spoken.

"Yeah, you can put your vagina away now, Lawrence," I snickered and gave in to the laughter, doubling over with giggles as Kate and I imitated the sincerity in his words.

Lawrence's smirk disolved and was replaced by a frowning grimace.

"Screw you," he muttered, dropping his head slightly and shoving his hands in his pockets, only causing us to laugh even harder.

"Oh crap," Kate panted, one hand over her stomach "I can't . . . breathe."

I continued giggling uncontrollably, but the look on Lawrence's face was becoming more and more sombre, so I tried to control my laughter by taking calming breaths. The same however, couldn't be said for Kate.

"Why couldn't you just say 'Dude, get these' rather than getting all pansy on me?" she snickered, wiping the tears from her eyes. She finally took a deep breath and straightened up with an evil smirk on her face. "Don't worry," she said, patting him on the shoulder, still smirking, "we won't tell anyone."

"Tell anyone what?"

My body stilled automatically as his gentle voice rang in my ears, shimmering in my mind and tingling in every nerve of my body. Knowing there was only one person who had this effect on me, I let out a small sigh as his scent engulfed me. I opened my mouth to speak but was stopped short by Lawrence.

"Nothing dude, don't listen to 'em," he said, giving Kate and me pointed glares that quite obviously said, "if you say anything I will kill you."

I smiled at him before chancing a peek at Kane, looking up at him through my lashes to find him smiling crookedly down at me, giving me a small wink that made my heart literally stop before running a sprint in my chest. Flashbacks of his lips molded to mine began attacking my mind, and I silently chided myself to get a grip.

I smiled back, but taking a closer look at his face, I couldn't help but frown. He had a crease in his forehead and dark shades under his eyes.

"You look tired," I whispered, frowning up at his face. My fingers twitched to touch him but I kept them to myself with much effort.

He stopped smiling at me and his face took on a defensive edge. Narrowing his eyes, his lips parted to speak whilst his eyes flashed with something that was too quick for me to distinguish. I stared back at him questioningly with a hint of concern, and a slight chuckle escaped his glorious form.

"Yeah, well, someone," he cocked an eyebrow at me meaning-fully before he continued, "kept me up until three in the morning," he mused mockingly with a smirk playing on the edges of his lips.

I blushed but smirked back, "Well, you don't seem to be complaining," I quipped, raising an eyebrow in return, earning a very sexy, very beautiful grin, which spread across his face, causing my breath to hitch. I bit my lip and watched, smugly, as his eyes flitted to my mouth and his warm, chocolate-brown eyes darkened slightly in color. A sudden clearing of the throat brought me back, and I realised that Kate and Lawrence were still present. I wasn't sure, but it seemed that Kane had been just as distracted as he blinked and refocused on his surroundings.

I turned to find the irritating culprit who pulled me out of my Kane Richards-daze only to find both Kate and Lawrence peering between Kane and me suspiciously. I bit my lip again and blushed faintly at the attention, causing Kane to chuckle throatily again.

"Dude we should probably go man, coach is all over me saying that I've been slacking. I need my main man to help me out a bit," Kane said, playfully punching Lawrence on the shoulder.

Lawrence merely nodded in reply, still glancing between us before shrugging and murmuring a quiet "catch you later" to Kate and me and heading off towards the gym.

I stared after him, and when I didn't immediately see Kane retreating I snapped my head up, only to find him staring at me intensely. His face was twisted in confusion and something near frustration, all the while keeping his eyes locked on my lips. He snapped out of it when a tall girl with copper hair and large gold earrings strutted up to him and placed a chaste kiss on his cheek.

"Hey, Kane," she purred in a voice that I supposed was her trying to sound seductive. I however found her voice rather repulsive but couldn't help the stab of jealousy that pierced through me. Then I remembered that it was me he was kissing for the first time since . . . God knows, and that it was my face he had cupped in his hands at two o'clock in the morning, and internally grinned at my smug thoughts.

I glared at her and wondered how Kane would blow her off. I ran through all the ways he could do it. Maybe just wince and push past her, or just give her a simple "Get lost." I actually smiled at that one. That seemed like him.

Only a moment had passed, and this . . . girl was still whispering huskily in his ear. His eyes were still locked on mine and I smiled smugly as I anticipated his reaction.

In a second flat my anticipation completely dissolved and my jaw hung loosely as Kane didn't push her away. He didn't pretend she didn't exist, and he definitely didn't tell her to get lost.

No.

Kane Richards put his arm possessively around her, and gazed down at her face, giving her the same crooked smile he gave me, causing her to giggle. Then they sauntered off down the hall without so much as a goodbye.

I stared at their retreating forms; livid and completely uncaring that Kate was still standing there and had witnessed the whole thing. I slammed my locker door shut and all but ran down the hall, leaving a bewildered Kate calling after me loudly.

As the angry tears spilled down my cheeks, I desperately tried to keep at bay the sobs that were threatening to rip through my torso. No way was I going to cry over him just like plenty of other girls had. He wasn't worthy of my tears, and yet, the image of him casually strolling down the hall away from me with his arm draped over someone else crushed my efforts; my walls fell down as I succumbed to the ebbing pain.

I was everything that Kate and Lawrence had told me not to become, and I had no one to blame but myself.

# 13. I'M SORRY

## Kane

I spotted Lawrence at the end of the hall talking to none other than that pain in the ass Kate, and there was a small figure next to them with her back to me who I couldn't quite make out.

As I dodged a couple of snotty bitches blatantly drooling at me from across the hall—had it been any other day I'd be lapping that shit up—I realized that the third figure was her. She didn't turn, and I didn't hear her voice, but I just knew it was her. I felt that same toxic magnetic pull she had on me.

And it was even stronger than it had been before.

I didn't understand my physical reactions at all. The hairs raised up on the back of my neck, I'm pretty sure my eyes dilated, my heart was going crazy, my fingers were feeling tingly, and why the hell was it so hot in here all of a sudden?

I felt like I was choking on the thickening air and took a deep breath to pull myself together, thinking of what to say when I got there. Luckily enough, Kate gave me the perfect opportunity when she put her hand on Lawrence's shoulder and murmured some shit about not telling anyone.

"Tell anyone what?" I asked, not really caring, but just using it as an excuse to hear Suranne speak. It had only been a few hours since I'd seen her, but she looked even better, and my eyes were eagerly lapping her up. I heard her sigh, and watched as her lips parted but then that cock-blocking Lawrence stopped whatever she was about to say.

"Nothing dude, don't listen to 'em," he muttered, glaring at them both. I don't know what the hell they were talking about, but I could see Suranne's lips twitch upward into a very small smirk and I couldn't help but grin. She was so sexy without even realizing it.

She peeked up at me through her lashes, and I grinned even wider as her gray eyes pierced right through me. I reminisced about how her eyes had shone when I was at her house, and I winked at her. Her eyes seemed to widen before they tightened infinitesimally as if she was trying to keep herself in check or some shit.

And I swear to God I almost lost it when her lips pulled up and she smiled widely at me.

Damn.

And I thought it was only Ashley's smile I loved seeing.

I would watch this girl smile all day if I could.

Her face puckered into a small frown, and her lips turned down at the edges as she eyed my face, concern now her main expression.

"You look tired," she whispered. I knew I looked like shit, but having it told to you doesn't really do much for your confidence. Then I felt pissed, because shit, you would be tired too if you walked in your home to find your Mom smashing glasses on the floor, completely wasted, and your sister bawling her eyes out in your room, wouldn't you?

But I couldn't feel completely angry, because the other reason that I didn't get much sleep was nowhere near as bad.

And so I chuckled, and decided to give her a little reminder.

"Yeah, well, someone kept me up till three in the morning," I told her suggestively, cocking an eyebrow, and was rewarded with a delicate blush coloring her cheeks.

I nearly groaned at the sight.

"Yeah, well, you don't seem to be complaining," she replied, her voice taking on a sly tone. I grinned back at her, because complaining was definitely something I wasn't going to do.

"Especially when you won't get the chance to do it again," I heard my mind say to itself, and just like that, I was reminded of the shit I'd been reluctant to do all morning. And when she bit her lip I couldn't help but divert my gaze to her mouth, wanting to do nothing more than lean in closer and kiss those damn lips till there was nothing left. When I forced my attention back to her eyes I was about to go crazy, completely lost in her stare. I gazed back, silently apologizing and willing her to understand.

Even though I knew she wouldn't. We were both brought back to reality by Lawrence clearing his throat, and inwardly I growled at him.

Like I said . . . cock-blocker.

Suranne snapped her head in his direction, and I decided to follow suit. Both he and Kate were looking at us suspiciously. Not that I gave a shit. I would quite happily let them watch if I was about to ravage her against her locker.

But I wasn't. I was going to screw everything up, and I didn't want to face the aftermath of Lawrence, grilling my ears off about how much of an asshole I am, and the smug look on Kate's face, either. I was about to ask if I could speak to her alone, and get this over and done with, but when she blushed, and bit her lip again, I just . . . couldn't. I couldn't do it. I needed to find another way around this shit. And I wouldn't be able to do that if she was there, right in front of me, all tantalizing and lip biting.

"Dude, we should probably go man, coach is all over me saying that I've been slacking. I need my main man to help me out a bit," I muttered to Lawrence, chuckling and punching his arm, 'cause if I didn't get away from her now, I would break down, tell her everything, and then push her against that damn wall and mash my lips against hers. But I knew I couldn't tell her about my mom, like I said before; she'd think of me as a dick. And even worse, she'd feel sorry for me.

And I don't need pity.

I was vaguely aware of Lawrence walking down the hall, and Suranne watching after him, but I was still focused on her lips. I didn't want to leave them, but if I kissed her now I'd have to explain shit and I didn't want to.

Lips and pity, or nothing at all?

And even though I was aware that the heavens up above enjoyed screwing around with my life, I didn't expect that they'd go all mercifully vengeful on my ass by sending some bronze-haired chick up to me to kiss me on the damn cheek.

And I knew it was stupid, and I was going to totally regret it, but after these two shitty days I came to the conclusion that to let people in is far more tiresome, frustrating, and downright scary than to push them away.

And just like that, lips and pity became a much worse scenario than nothing at all, and I desperately tried to communicate this to Suranne using my eyes, apologizing and hoping that by some miracle she'd be able to read my mind. But she seemed far more amused with the chick hanging on my arm than anything else, and so with one last look at her lips, I did what was easiest for me. I pushed her away. And when I put my arm around the chick I didn't even know, and saw Suranne's jaw drop, and her face twist in what could only be pain, I knew that maybe I'd pushed her a bit too far, and that there would be no going back.

So I turned away from her, and got the hell out of there, 'cause there was nothing else I could do. With every step I took, my chest ached more to go back. But I kept walking, with only two words prominent in my mind.

I'm sorry.

# 14. THOUGHTLESS PAYBACK

## Suzanne

After a whole bloody hour of trying to pull myself together, and wiping the tears off my cheeks, I took a deep breath, crossed the field and made my way back into the school building. Second lesson was approaching, which was biology, and luckily Kane wouldn't be in my class. He was the last person I wanted to see right now.

I heard the first bell ring and quickened my pace, trying to reach the class door. As I walked through the halls, the other students were eyeing me, half of the girls looking smug, before turning to their friends and yammering quietly, and the other half just looking at me with pity in their eyes. News obviously got around that the new little British girl fell for the famous antics of Kane Richards, and everyone was making quick work of the latest gossip.

In my haste to reach class I arrived early and the only other person in the room, thankfully, was Lawrence. He had his head in his hands, elbows on the desk, and seemed to be silently muttering to himself. I walked quietly up to him, and placed my hand gently on his shoulder but was shocked when I felt him stiffen underneath me and shake my hand off as if he was disgusted to have me even touching him.

"Lawrence?" I questioned warily, but he just cringed at hearing my voice, then finally turned to face me. However, this time it was my turn to cringe.

73

Lawrence looked angry. But not just an "I'm pissed off" kind of angry.

No.

It was much worse than that. This was a broken, disappointed, and rejected "how could you" kind of angry, and from the looks of it, it seemed to be directed straight at me.

"You just don't listen, do you?" he glared, his warm, ocean-blue eyes now transformed into a cold, icy blue that was considerably darker than the norm.

"You just . . . don't . . . get," he trailed off, sighing and shaking his head before holding it in his hands once again. I stood there with the hand that had been on his shoulder still hovering slightly, my eyes wide and my body stiff from the shock of his words as he continued speaking menacingly, his voice sounding low and hollow from his head being surrounded by his hands.

"We told you, the first day, Kate and I TOLD you what he was like, and you . . . you just. Don't. Damn. Well. Listen." He sneered at me, his voice sharp, cutting through me.

I stood there, blinking uncontrollably whilst his words swirled around in my head.

"Lawrence . . . I—I . . . it wasn't even . . . I . . . ." I stuttered. It was impossible to even think coherently so speech was definitely out of the question. He was right, I knew I should have listened to them both and just ignored Kane, but I honestly felt that I had witnessed a different side of him, and he said he didn't compare me to his past girls.

He said I wasn't like them

He said I was different.

He said I was better

He also *kissed* me.

Then he chucked me like I was nothing.

I wonder how many other girls he had used the same lines on, just to get them to drop their pants.

I wanted to say all of this to him, but for some strange reason there was something buried deep within me that also wanted to defend him, even after he'd worked me over. I wanted to yell and cry and scream that Kane isn't what everyone thinks he is.

But how could I?

He just proved everyone right not an hour ago.

And now everyone was laughing and sneering behind my back. Hell, Kane was probably one of them, bragging how he had me hook, line, and sinker, before something else came along. This was apparently a copper-headed, gold hoop-wearing, trout-smelling bitch.

As if that wasn't enough, Kate was probably just as mad as Lawrence was, and if I thought he was bad when he was angry, he had nothing on Kate.

Damn.

And so the tears started silently running again because all I wanted to do now was just get a ring from my mum telling me she had arrived back so I could catch the first available plane and get the hell out of there. Leave all this behind me and forget it even existed. Go back to my real home, call my real friends, flop down on my real bed, walk to the fish and chip shop and have some real food, and guzzle a ton of Red Bull. Go to college like I was supposed to, meet a decent guy who was nice, and friendly, and gentle, and caring, and much better looking than Kane.

Pshh . . . Who was I kidding? There was no one better looking than Kane. Perfection doesn't do his looks justice. He was much more than perfect.

Lawrence's eyes widened and he sighed. "Suranne, I'm sorry. I didn't mean to make you cry, I just," he ducked his head and kept his eyes on the floor, "I thought you were different," he muttered.

"Lawrence I don't know what you think is going on between Kane and me but I can assure you I haven't done anything with him."

Apart from kiss him in the early hours of the morning. And fantasise about him constantly.

His head snapped up and he looked at me in shock.

"You haven't had sex with him?"

In my mind? Definitely.

"Uhh, no," I replied, shifting my eyes from side to side, hoping that my blush wouldn't betray me and my nightly dreams.

He seemed to believe me and he sighed in relief. His mouth spread into a wide grin and he patted the chair next to him as the class began to slowly fill up with students. I sat down next to him appreciatively and smiled back. "I'm sorry about what I said," he murmured, his blue eyes warm and shining again as they gazed into mine.

"It's OK." I smiled back at him and he raised his hand slowly, brushing the tears away from my cheeks softly with the pad of his thumb. His eyes flitted to my lips for a few seconds before the teacher came in, and he reluctantly pulled away from me.

The day followed on sluggishly for me after that. At the end of every lesson my chest tightened and my heart thudded in my chest from the thought of running into Kane in the halls.

I never did, and for that I was grateful.

I did, however, have Lawrence escort me to all of my classes and was glad that he was here for me. I could tell from all the stares and the sideways glances from other people that, unlike them, Lawrence didn't judge me anymore. But unlike them, he knew I hadn't had sex with Kane Richards. They didn't.

The bell rang to signal the end of school and I breathed a sigh of relief as I was met at the door by Lawrence, his bright blue eyes gleaming and a wide grin that, if Kane hadn't existed, would count as being extremely sexy. He slung his arm around my shoulder and we made our way into the parking lot. I had accepted a ride home with him at lunch in the hope that I wouldn't run into Kane.

I was taking no chances.

"So, Suranne, uhh, I was wondering, if umm, maybe, I don't know, I just guess I would like it if you came back to my place and we hung out for a while. Kate's always with us and I think it would be pretty cool if it was you and me," Lawrence stuttered as I leaned against the passenger door and he leaned over me, his arm resting on the roof of his car, next to my head.

"Uh, sure," I said absently, my eyes flitting around the lot, subconsciously looking for Kane. If I could get him on his own maybe I could scream at him and possibly spit in his too-beautiful face.

Or maybe kiss him again? Wait, what? Where the hell did that come from?

"Hey," I heard Lawrence murmur whilst his hand cupped my chin and pulled me to face him. "You still with me? Looked like you were miles away."

My breathing sped up as his eyes darted to my lips, his breathing heavy and warm against my face as he leaned in closer.

"Suranne," he whispered quietly and before I got the chance to respond, his lips came dangerously close to mine, desperate and wanting. His hand snaked into my hair and held my face to his.

"What the fuck is this?!" I heard a familiar voice next to us exclaim and Lawrence quickly pulled away.

I turned my head to the side slightly and smirked.

Hi, Kane.

# 15. REALIZATIONS

## Kane

**M**y fists clenched at my sides. No way in hell was Lawrence kissing her.

My girl. Whether she liked it or not.

Yeah, I felt guilty about earlier today, but shit. The fact that Suranne just stood there smirking at me didn't help. And Lawrence, slightly breathless, looking at me like I was an idiot for interrupting him.

Too bad.

I grabbed Suranne's arm and dragged her across the lot towards my car, ignoring her attempts to pull away from me, and ignoring Lawrence calling after us. Right now I really didn't give a shit what either of them wanted. The ache in my chest had increased tenfold, and just watching them had boiled my blood. I can't remember the last time I felt so angry over a girl. Well, maybe I can, but I'm not going there.

"What are you doing?!" she yelled at me as I tugged her roughly behind me, completely ignoring her. I couldn't deal with this crap. As we approached the door to my car, I pulled her roughly and spun her around so that she was pressed up against the door. I didn't let go of her hand, instead I grasped the other one as well so that both her hands were tightly in mine. I pushed up against her roughly.

"What the *hell* was all that about, huh?" My voice was low and cold while I tried to rein in my anger, and if I was completely honest, my jealousy as well. I cocked an eyebrow, waiting for her to speak, but she just continued staring into my eyes, her breathing becoming labored and heavy. I came undone when she bit her lip and all my blood rushed down to my groin.

Groaning quietly, I dropped my head.

"What's wrong, Kane? Don't you like someone messing around with you like you do with them? Bit hypocritical don't you think?" she sneered at me, a slight vindictive smirk tugging at her lips.

"That's completely different," I spat sharply. "I wasn't kissing the goddamn girl in front of you was I?!"

"You didn't need to!" she snarled back at me, and I noticed her gray eyes flashing in anger and in . . . vulnerability? I wasn't sure, but I knew that she was hiding something from me. Seeing as I was doing the same thing, I let it go.

"You don't understand . . . I . . . can't . . . right . . . now," I mumbled, dropping my gaze to the ground, half wanting her to hear me, and half not wanting her to. I heard her huff in exasperation, and snapped my head to look up at her.

"You're bloody well right I don't understand!" she yelled at me, her sexy-ass accent coming out thicker, and only making my hard-on worse. I could feel myself straining against my pants to the point where it was almost uncomfortable.

"And seeing as you're obviously not going to explain it to me, you can let go and leave me to my own devices," she continued, her eyes shining smugly, "including Lawrence."

I could tell she was waiting for a reaction from me, and what d'you know, it worked. My eyes narrowed, my fists clenched around hers and two words burned in my thoughts.

*You're mine.*

She smirked as she saw my anger, obviously happy that she got the reaction she wanted. Not caring, I pressed harder up against her, ducking my head so that I could whisper roughly into her ear.

"Is this what you want, Suranne, huh? Do you know what you do to me?" I groaned, and pushed my hips roughly into hers, getting a gasp and a low whimper in response. She dropped her head to my shoulder as her body became limp against mine and I thought about how much I affected her, a smug grin on my face.

After a couple of seconds of her heavy panting on my shoulder, her hot breath burning through the fabric to my skin, she regained some of her strength and tugged against my hands slightly, trying to get free. I held on tighter.

"Why can't you just let me go?" she whimpered, and I could tell by the tone of her voice that she wasn't just talking about my hands. I wished so badly that I could just tell her, but the more selfish part of my head was stronger than the confident part at the moment. So I stayed silent, squeezing my eyes shut, and wishing I could man up and get some courage. When I opened my eyes and finally focused on our surroundings I noticed that people had actually stopped midstep to stare at both of us, all wide-eyed and whispering. I could see all the chicks looked pretty angry, including the red-headed chick that I had walked away with earlier. As bad as I had felt about Suranne, I'd needed some release to get my stress levels down so I'd let her lead me off to the janitor's closet.

But the whole time I was thinking about how Suranne's face had twisted in pain when I had hooked my arm around the other chick. I just couldn't erase the pictures from my head. And the burning ache in my chest only got worse as soon as she got down on her knees. After a while I just got pissed off, pushed her off me, and walked to class.

"People are looking Kane, please, just let me go," Suranne pleaded, the last three words strained as her voice broke slightly, like she didn't have the strength anymore.

*No, Suranne, please just wait for me.*

But my body let her go and she stumbled away from me, sniffling quietly and treading unsteadily back to Lawrence's car as he glared daggers at me and put his arm possessively around her.

Whatever.

I spied the rest of the lot and noticed that all eyes seemed to follow Suranne's movements until Lawrence's car peeled out of the lot. Then their eyes snapped back to mine.

"Fuck off," I muttered lowly as I got into my car and started the engine. The familiar growl permeated through the small space. I put the car in gear and screeched out of there as the eyes of the entire school burned into my mirrors before disappearing altogether.

I realized that for once, the guys weren't cheering and murmuring about how I was the man. They were looking at me like I was crazy. Like I had somehow lost my touch, no longer desired by the entire female population.

At that moment, as I came back to focusing on the road in front of me, I knew that when I returned to school tomorrow, I was no longer going to be *the* Kane Richards. And if it meant that I would be able to get my girl in the process, then it meant that I really didn't give a shit.

# 16. TEXT MESSAGES

## Suranne

The car was silent apart from our breathing and the occasional sniffle from me. Lawrence fiddled with the radio for a while, but didn't find a station that appealed to him, so he turned it off.

After a few more minutes of silence, he turned to me slightly. "Suranne, are you OK?" he asked softly, turning his head back to the road and then glancing at me quickly.

I nodded absently, my mind still thinking about how my whole jealousy payback thing had backfired. For some reason Kane always seemed to have the upper hand.

"So, what do you wanna do once we reach my place?" he asked lightly, trying to remove the dark cloud that had filled the space between us. Shaken out of my daze my head snapped up, my tone of voice instantly contrite.

"Oh crap, Lawrence, I'm so sorry but . . . would you mind just taking me home?" I pleaded softly.

He turned towards me, shocked, before concentrating back on the road. "But . . . you said—"

"I know Lawrence, but . . . please . . . I just really wanna go home." Tears slowly started to gather at the corners of my eyes again.

"OK," he sighed heavily, and took the next turn towards my aunt's. I hung my head, now feeling guilty that I had been leading Lawrence on just because of Kane. It was cruel and he deserved someone so much better.

"I'm sorry," I whispered softly, looking out the window, wiping the new tears that slid silently down my cheeks.

"Hey," he murmured, lifting one hand and cupping my chin, turning it towards him so that he could look at my face.

"Don't worry, Suranne, I'm not gonna push you. If you want me as a friend, then that's who I'll be," he assured. But I could see the sadness and rejection shining in his blue eyes. Lawrence was amazing and the sane part of me wished that it was his blue eyes I thought about daily instead of warm chocolate-brown ones. Wished that there was some part of me that could feel attracted to him, even if it was only small, so that it could build up over time.

But there was nothing.

Nothing except brown eyes, and sweet-fragranced cologne, and the smooth velvet voice that made my ears sigh in contentment.

There was nothing but Kane.

And I hated it.

I gave him a weak smile of gratitude, turned my face to look out the window, and thought back to when Kane had me pushed up against his car. How my breath had hitched and my pulse had quickened when he whispered in my ear. How I felt a jolt of desire race through my veins every time he had pushed his hips into mine, and how the sound of his groan drove me wild. How his touch left a trail of tingling fire burning on my skin. How his sweet scent engulfed me and left my mind blank and reeling.

He said I didn't know what I did to him, but if it was anything like what he did to me then I definitely knew.

I knew too well.

Lawrence pulled me out of my reverie when he switched off the engine.

"Alright, we're here," he announced, keeping his hands firmly locked on the steering wheel. I bobbed my head and hummed as the air between us became awkward. Lawrence shifted in his seat nervously before he sighed and turned his shoulders towards me.

"Just . . . one time, Suranne," he pleaded softly before abruptly shifting forward and gently pressing his lips to mine. He sighed into my mouth, cradling my face in his hands as my whole body stayed frozen. He broke the kiss only to give me smaller chaste ones against my lips and the edge of my mouth.

"OK," he sighed, pulling away and putting his hands back on the steering wheel. "I'll be OK now." He nodded and I blinked stiffly at him, then stepped out of the car and walked into my house without a backward glance. My aunt greeted me from across the living room and I gave her a weak smile, walking past her and heading up the stairs. Once I reached my bedroom and flopped down on the bed, I closed my eyes and covered my face with my hands. Lawrence's lips never gave me that jolt of electricity that Kane's had. My lips still felt the same as they always did.

With a groan of frustration I rolled over, pressing my face into the pillow. I felt a vibration against my left thigh and jumped, pulling my phone out of my pocket.

One new text message from Kate.

*Hey, heard Kane got to you aftr skl. U Ok? xKx*

I sighed and pressed the reply button.

*Yeah, im fine. Just feeling rly confsd — S*

After a few seconds my phone buzzed again.

*Dnt wrry, he does tht to evry1. Heard u didn't cave tho. Im proud xKx*

I grimaced at that. If only she knew.

*Its Lawr. Im more worried abwt. He lukd rly upset t.day –S*

*He'll get over it. I'm sure he'll find sum1 at the flowrshop LOL xKx*

I giggled as I looked at the screen, remembering Lawrence's knowledge of flowers. As I pressed the reply button and began typing out my first word, my phone buzzed again.

"God, give me a chance," I mumbled to myself, rolling my eyes. It buzzed again and I growled at her impatience whilst I exited my created message and went into my inbox.

Two new text messages.

MEET ME
I'LL EXPLAIN EVERYTHING

I frowned at my phone, staring dumbly at the two text messages. Kate never texted in capitals and she always left her classic "xKx" signature. I couldn't think of anyone else who had my number and wouldn't leave their name. Lawrence always rang, saying that texting was overrated, and my aunt was downstairs.

I looked at the number and didn't recognise it. Pressing the reply button I started tapping at the keys.

*Who is this? – S*

I waited anxiously and immediately grabbed my phone once it started buzzing.

THE SAME PERSON WHO WATCHED YOU AIRPLAY YIRUMA'S RIVER FLOWS IN YOU AND THOUGHT YOU LOOKED HOT DOING IT

My breathing stopped, my phone slipped from my grasp, and my heart thudded in my chest, my eyes wide in recognition.

Kane.

How the hell did he get my number?

Before I had the chance to mull over the question properly in my mind my phone buzzed again from the floor. I leaned over and grabbed it, flipping it open and reading the new text message.

MEET ME @ THE SAME BENCH IN HALF HOUR?

It was a question. I didn't have to say yes, I didn't have to be entranced by his lean, sexy body and his hair and his voice and his warm eyes and his too sweet smell.

I didn't have to.

And yet, when I glanced down at my phone, I saw that my fingers had already tapped out my reply.

*I'll Be There.*

# 17. TRUST

## Suranne

I reached the secluded bench and sat down to that same cool breeze blowing around me. I wrapped my arms around my torso, hugging myself whilst I glanced at the calm, still scenery in front of me.

Every few seconds my eyes darted from left to right. I couldn't help the buildup of nerves that had settled in the pit of my stomach, but I'd needed to come. He said he was going to explain everything, and I deserved an explanation.

I felt my phone buzzing in my pocket and pulled it out, staring at it curiously. I flipped it open, and frowned at the screen.

One new text message. From the same number as before.

CLOSE YOUR EYES

I turned around and peered between the trees and bushes trying to spot him, squinting as my eyes flitted in different directions. My phone buzzed again and I looked down at the screen.

THEY'RE NOT CLOSED SURANNE

I sighed in frustration, unable to see him anywhere yet he could quite obviously see me. After a while I relented, with a defeated sigh, and turned back around, slumping against the bench. I closed my eyes hesitantly. I tried to control my breathing as my inner excitement grew at the thought of seeing him, hearing his voice, gazing into those brown eyes again. I had seen him not more than two hours ago, and I deeply missed him already.

After a couple of seconds a familiar smell assaulted my senses. I felt a sudden rush of feeling like I was back at home, in London. The scent was unforgettable, rich and mouthwatering. It was a scent I hadn't indulged in for far too long.

Fish and chips.

A small moan escaped my lips as the smell became stronger and my stomach growled furiously. My eyes snapped open of their own volition and I was rewarded with a beautiful sight.

"If you had any idea how fucking impossible it was to get this, I think you'd love me just that much more." He smiled crookedly at me, dressed in the same outfit he was in when I first saw him. Snugly fitted black button-down shirt and dark jeans, the front of his hair spiked up neatly as always, his deep brown eyes shining brightly, and his little sexy stud in his ear.

I didn't know what I wanted more. The food or him.

"How did you know?" I breathed, reaching out for the food. It was even wrapped in paper like it was back home and I smiled broadly at his efforts. As far as I knew shops like that didn't even exist here.

"I know it's the national dish or some shit, I figured you'd be into it. I guess I'm right, huh?" He shrugged, sitting down next to me and watching with a smirk on his face as I greedily tucked in. After a while I felt a little bit self-conscious stuffing my face whilst he was watching me, so I started eating it more slowly. He seemed to notice my hesitance and laughed lowly before leaning over and whispering in my ear, his silky voice washing through my brain and leaving a pool of uncoordinated mess in its wake.

"Just for the record, the sight of you eating is extremely sexy, Suranne. Don't stop."

I gulped at his words and his voice before a question struck me.

"How the bloody hell did you get my number, Kane? First it's my address and now this. Anyone would think you're stalking me." I looked at him with raised eyebrows before popping another couple of chips in my mouth, nearly groaning at the taste. They weren't quite as good as home's, but they were a close second.

He shrugged and smiled at me.

"I have my ways."

I swallowed and nodded, saving that answer for later. Right now I wanted what he promised me.

An explanation.

I put the chips down between us and wiped my hands, turning fully to him and raising my eyebrows in question. He seemed to realise what I wanted right away and cringed, throwing his head back and groaning up at the sky.

"You want the explanation, am I right?" he muttered.

"Well, it would be nice," I chuckled dryly, folding my arms over my chest, but otherwise keeping silent, waiting for him to explain it in his own time. I guessed there was more to it than "I just really want to screw you."

He lifted his head and turned to me reluctantly. Closing his eyes, his face turned into a grimace before he lifted his chin slightly in determination and squared his shoulders. He opened his eyes and looked levelly at me and as I gazed back at him, I saw the defeat evident in his stare. After a few moments of us gazing at each other, his full, soft lips parted to speak, and he graced me with his heavenly voice.

"For you to really get all this, I'll just have to start at the beginning," he mumbled, his face twisted and his voice low and ragged. My hand ached to touch him. I had never seen him showing such emotion before, not just to me but to anyone, and I immediately wanted to alleviate it. Taking another deep breath, he stared intensely at me. A stare that told me this was difficult for him. That he hadn't talked about this in a long time, and that at this moment in time, he trusted me. I smiled reassuringly and gave him an encouraging nod.

"My father was the managing partner of a law firm. When it came to his line of work, he was expected to host large dinner parties and attend important events overseas with different companies. He had a lot of friends and whenever he held dinner parties the smile on his face was never fake." His jaw clenched and he squinted his eyes tightly before his face relaxed.

"He was also a proud man. Proud of his wife, his son, his daughter, his home, his job, and the amount of work he put into the firm. And he was always generous with money, hosting different social events to fund charities and shit. He set up trust funds for each of us, always chucking ridiculous amounts of money into them for no reason. I used some of mine to buy my car and it hardly put a dent in my balance." A heavy sigh escaped him as he shook his head. "His firm is still going strong, and the money now goes directly to us. Well . . . mainly to my mom." His fists clenched in his lap when he mentioned his mother and he averted his gaze over my shoulder, narrowing his eyes at the various trees, shrubs, and our surroundings in general, before continuing.

"Three years ago, my father had to attend a social event in Hong Kong. He took a private jet; he said that it was always easier for him," he muttered darkly. I kept watching him, transfixed with how the different emotions played across his face. Hurt. Anger. Guilt. Reluctance.

Although some part of it scared me, there was a much larger part that kept me intrigued with the new side of him that he was letting me discover. His large, alluring brown eyes glazed over with a faraway look, as if he were completely involved in a memory of some kind. He spoke as if in a trance.

"The plane crashed that night," he whispered. I inhaled a sharp breath, my eyes wide, and my jaw dropped slightly. Deep down I had guessed where this story was leading. I could tell from the hurt that was evident on his face, but the bluntness with which Kane said it shocked me.

I reached out to touch his arm in apology and he snatched it away from me, his blank chocolate eyes flashing in anger.

"I don't want your pity!" he spat at me sharply. I recoiled from the tone in his voice, leaning back away from him and putting my hand back on my lap.

He sighed and ran his hand through his hair muttering to himself.

"Shit . . . it's why I didn't wanna do this shit . . ."

I tried making sense of his jumbled words but couldn't come up with anything, and didn't particularly want to ask him when he was in this mood, so I just sat there silently. After a few minutes of tense silence and Kane constantly running his hand through his hair, causing it to become a dishevelled but sexy mess, he dropped his head in his hands and groaned slightly.

"I'm sorry . . . I just . . . damn . . . I'm not good with words," he mumbled awkwardly. I nodded slowly in response, still wary of his outburst yet still wanting to touch him. He raised his head slowly and his eyes locked with mine. They burned and swirled with such intense emotions that I nearly gasped out loud. I had never seen Kane look like this, and I had never wanted him more.

He scooted closer to me and placed a hand on my cheek. His blazing eyes were still locked on mine, not allowing me to escape the intensity of his stare.

I could see his hesitation. He wanted to get this off his chest, and yet I could also see his fear, his apprehension, and I knew I had to put him at ease. I leaned into his touch and pressed my forehead against his, our eyes still locked and unmoving. His stare begged for understanding, my stare begged for trust.

"Trust me, Kane," I whispered, closing my eyes and leaning my face closer. I was giving him the only thing I could, and the only thing I knew would help.

"Trust me," I murmured once again, before pressing my lips softly to his, still keeping my eyes closed, too afraid to see the expression in his. In my mind, I realised that this could only go one of two ways. Either I was doing the right thing and Kane would appreciate my form of appeasement, and hopefully kiss me back, or he would misjudge my actions as a sign of sympathy and withdraw from me altogether, possibly leaving at the same time.

This was my only chance, and I fervently hoped that I had made the right decision.

## 18. PAINFUL MEMORIES

### Kane

"Trust me," she whispered against my lips before brushing hers lightly against mine. I felt the same fleck of electricity go through my lips and down my body as the last time I'd kissed her. Sighing into her mouth I lifted my other hand, cupping her face as my lips moved with hers. I needed this right now, and she seemed to know. The hold this girl had over me was baffling at the best of times. But at times like this I was glad for that shit. When I had gone home earlier that day, I'd tried once again to get my mind off of her through other chicks. I thought about calling a hot blonde to let her try all her best techniques on me but that wouldn't suffice.

I needed her. Suranne.

Even if my mind wanted to deny it, there was no denying the fact that my body wanted her.

And only her.

I knew that meant I had to go all out. I had to man up and tell her shit that I hadn't told anyone. Well, apart from that other bitch . . . but she just—

No, Kane. Don't go there.

I knew this was going to be difficult and tried to prepare myself as best I could. Allowing my mind to drift back to the place I had pushed away for so many years ripped a painful hole through me. And it was just at that moment Suranne decided to put her hand on my arm. The whole reason why I didn't want to tell people in the first place was because I didn't want to see the sympathy and pity in their eyes.

I shouldn't have snapped at her but hell, I couldn't help it, and then I knew it was over, and I had blown it. I sounded like a dick and I was expecting her to run away just like the other bitch had. To leave me dealing with this crap on my own.

Again.

But she stayed.

Jesus Christ, she stayed.

She took her hand away, and she sat there . . . silently . . . waiting.

For me.

Had this been any other day I would have been grinning from ear to ear at that. But the pain I was in had such a strong hold on me from being kept inside all these years that now, as I let it out, it became its own force, rearing out and swallowing me whole. The pain in my chest and in my mind was taking over and I needed her to understand. I needed her to help. I needed her to reassure me that she'll be there once she realizes how messed up I am. I needed her to accept me, and the shitload of baggage that was my life.

I just needed her, period.

Her kiss told me everything I needed to know. Her kiss told me she trusted me, that she wasn't leaving yet, and that she needed me as well.

It told me that she was mine, and that once I told her everything, I would be hers, too.

But I knew that already. I guess deep down I should have known that I had become hers the second I saw her face. I shouldn't have tried so hard to fight it.

I pulled away from her, still cupping her face in my hands and gave her a weak smile. The pain of my father's death was still wracking through me, making it difficult to breathe. But I was still gonna try and smile at my girl. She deserved it.

"I trust you," I murmured, silently thanking her through my eyes. Taking a deep breath I sat back, letting the memories of that night wash through me and possess every bone in my body. I wasn't even aware that I was speaking, could hardly feel my lips moving, but I knew they were. The only thing that was happening in my mind was that night.

All over again.

"Hey Dad, what's up?" I had said lightly over the phone. The line was weak and crackling, but I could hear his heavy breathing.

"Kane, look after your mother and your sister, son. Don't let anything or anyone distract you from them, y'hear?" he wheezed, the noise of other voices shouting rang through the line.

"Dad, what's going on? Who's shouting in the background? . . . Dad?!" The line crackled more and my heart thumped unevenly as my chest constricted. I glanced at the clock, it was nearly midnight. He'd be over the ocean now.

"Put me on loudspeaker, son . . ." Dad croaked amongst the shouting and crying I could hear in the background. I yelled for Mom to come into the living room, and she ran in, followed by a nine-year-old Ash, eyes all wide and anxious.

I put the phone on loudspeaker and the room abruptly filled with the sounds of crying, wailing, and my father's heavy breathing. Every few seconds the line would crackle and cut out before reconnecting.

"Sal?" My father cried. "Something's wrong with the plane . .
I don't know if I'll be home . . . Kiss Ash goodnight for me,
sweetheart." We could hear his voice break at the mention of Ash.
My mom burst into an uncontrollable fit of tears, while I
clenched my jaw, gripping the phone tightly, praying over and
over that I wasn't about to lose my father.

"Tell her I love her," he croaked thickly, and I could sense he
was crying. That pushed my mother over the edge and she fell to
her knees, sobbing into her hands. I refused to accept what I
knew was happening.

"What the hell is going on?!" I spat angrily through my teeth,
failing at my attempts to control my fear and pain.

"I'm right here, Dad," Ash sniffled in a small voice, coming
up to me. I wrapped an arm around her tightly, closing my eyes
as my father's broken voice filled the room again.

"Oh, Ash, baby, don't cry, Mommy and Kane are gonna look
after you now. You make sure you're good for them, OK?"

I totally lost it when he said that, so my mom weakly lifted
herself off the floor and snatched the phone out of my hands.
"Daniel, please don't!" she begged into the receiver, sobbing and
hiccupping. I kneeled down and held onto Ash as she sobbed into
my shoulder and my own tears fell into her hair.

"Sally . . . baby, don't worry," his sniffled words echoed into
the living room and fell over our lifeless, sobbing bodies.

"I can't do it on my own, Daniel!" my mother wailed and my
father let out a weak, broken laugh.

"Don't be silly, you're a beautiful, wonderful mom. Funny,
soft, gentle, smart, delicate . . . I love you. Please don't give up on

them, baby, they need you. I love you, always have, and always will."

The screams in the background got even louder and they ricocheted off the living room walls.

"Dad. . . just . . . I don't know, can't they fucking *do something*?" I exclaimed, angry that he was on the phone talking to us and saying goodbye when he could be using it to save his life.

"Kane, I've told you about your swearing. Stop setting a bad example. Be gentle on your mother, OK? Make me proud, son . . . " Those were his last words before the phone made a high-pitched noise and the line went dead.

Silence.

The room was thrown into an eerie silence, before the reality of what just happened dawned on us, and all three of us broke down simultaneously. Mom threw the phone at the wall, and Ash and I watched numbly as it crashed into a million plastic pieces. Then she broke down again, slumping on the floor, and clutching her chest tightly.

As her grieving wails filled the room, my father's last words rang through my mind with perfect clarity over and over.

Make me proud, son.

Make me proud.

My eyes focused once again on the greenery surrounding the bench, and I remained silent as I came back to the present. I was suddenly aware that the wind was blowing across my face, drying the tears that hadn't been shed since that night. I swiped them away quickly, and sniffed, folding my arms over my chest, unwilling to look in Suranne's direction. I braced myself for the two words which had became the worst part of telling someone your father died. Those two words had tainted my shitty life, and if she said them I knew I would just explode. People always felt the need to say "I'm sorry," when I said I didn't have a father, and every time I had to rein in my anger.

"Thank you," she whispered into the air and my head snapped in her direction, my eyes immediately locking onto her face. I let out a heavy breath which I hadn't realized I had been holding when I noticed that her expression wasn't one of apology, sympathy, or pity.

It was one of gratitude.

She slid up next to me, and pressed her hands firmly to my face, forcing me to look at her as she spoke in a determined voice, her eyes confident. "After what you did just now, Kane . . . I'd say your father would most definitely be proud of his son," she murmured. I wanted to cry again, and hold onto her for the rest of my life. No one had ever said anything more healing to me. I felt my whole body warm towards her, and I smiled weakly as her words hung in the air, repairing the huge mess that was left in my body from the pain of telling her that story.

I had never felt such relief and took her hand, pulling her up against me so her body was flush against mine. I wrapped my arms tightly around her and pressed my lips to hers once before I pulled away and sighed in contentment.

"Thank you," I murmured into her hair as I tightened my hold on her and inhaled her irresistible scent.

# 19. THE CALM BEFORE THE STORM

## Suzanne

"I disagree, I think that Beethoven's "Moonlight Sonata" also refers to women's beauty, and their luminosity, not to mention their ever-changing temperaments. I think it portrays hope, love, loss, and sadness all in one," I argued.

For a couple of hours we had been sitting there, or rather lying there lazily sipping from our bottles; I was casually sprawled across his chest as we talked about some of the greatest compositions.

After Kane told me what happened to his father, I knew that there was nothing that would stop me from loving him. I had felt such a wave of immense pride and gratitude that he had trusted me, let go, and opened himself up. Trusted me so deeply that he even let me see him cry, see how vulnerable he actually was.

He had held me for a few minutes before he mentioned that he was hungry and we went to get some Chinese and some fizzy drinks before returning back to our spot. We opted for the ground instead of the bench and Kane retrieved a blanket from the boot of his car, spreading it across the grass before we dug in to our food.

"Yeah, right!" Kane scoffed, "Why does everything have to lead back to women? Why can't it just portray the beauty of the moonlight?"

"Because it has too much of a romantic edge to it to just be about the moon, Kane," I sighed. "Have some perspective, man."

"I agree that there is . . . something romantic about it. But then sometimes anything to do with the moon can connote signs of some . . . romanticism shit," he replied nonchalantly.

"Yes, I'm sure that when Beethoven composed his piece he, too, agreed that there were indeed some signs of *romanticism shit*," I snickered, only to be playfully swatted on the arse by Kane.

"I think that last remark was uncalled for, Miss Williams," he stated in a low husky voice, before removing my bottle of drink and setting it on the ground next to him, only to roll us both over so that he was hovering over me slightly, holding himself up on his elbows. "You're beautiful," he whispered, his breath lightly fanning across my face. Then he ducked his head and brushed his lips gently against mine. I wrapped my arms around his neck and deepened the kiss, eliciting a low moan from him, and parted my lips, granting his tongue entrance as it explored my mouth.

"Damn it . . . Suranne . . ." he rasped in between kisses, "You're so hot, I can't deal with this shit." He moaned against my neck, licking towards my collar bone. The feel of his lips on my skin drove me wild with lust. Kane grunted roughly just as I felt a familiar buzzing in my jean pocket. I groaned in frustration and Kane rolled off of me, his breathing heavy, and his eyes considerably darker as he watched me take out my phone.

I flipped it open and was greeted with my aunt's voice. "Where in the world are you?! One minute you're home and then the next you're just gone!"

I rolled my eyes and mouthed "My aunt" at Kane, to which he sighed and nodded before I spoke into the receiver.

"I did actually tell you I was going out, but you were too engrossed in your cooking show," I replied nonchalantly. My eyes flickered to Kane instinctively and I bit my lip as I took in his ruffled hair, his swollen lips, and his creased black shirt.

". . . and I just don't know what to do with you these days."

I remembered that I was in fact in a conversation with my aunt, but Kane had distracted me from what she had been saying.

"Sorry, what?" I asked, blinking and trying to concentrate. But every time she spoke, my eyes ended up unabashedly creeping back to him. After the fourth time, Kane smiled crookedly at me and chuckled as he ran a hand through his hair before he snatched the phone and pressed it to his ear.

"I'm sorry to bother you, Miss Williams; it is my fault that Suranne has been distracted lately. I will be driving her home shortly." The words slid off his tongue like melted butter and his velvet voice once again hugged my ears as he spoke to my aunt reassuringly. I couldn't concentrate on their conversation. My eyes were still surveying every inch of his body, from his creased and rumpled black shirt, to his jeans, which were falling low on his hips. A sliver of his stomach was peeking out and I could just make out the soft brown hairs of his happy trail as it disappeared underneath his jeans.

My breathing had become heavy and my eyes were transfixed.

Out of nowhere I was pushed down onto my back and Kane was on top of me, looking deeply into my eyes.

"How the hell can I think clearly when you're looking at me like that?" he questioned huskily into my ear. I was too breathless to form a response. He chuckled and lifted his head, pressing his lips down onto mine, kissing me hungrily as he fisted his hands in my hair. I moaned quietly as his lips moved against mine before he broke the kiss and rolled off of me again.

"Come on, time to go," he said, his voice still rough, and his eyes still dark as he started cleaning up the empty Chinese containers.

"Oh, but why?" I whined, pouting up at him with a reluctant look on my face. He turned his head to look at me and his lips parted to speak. But as he took in my expression his face softened, and he smiled down at me before leaning down and kissing me sweetly. He held out a hand to help me up. "Because I promised your aunt that I would get you home safely, and before seven, and it's now . . ." He dug into his pockets for his phone and glanced at it briefly "Six forty-five." I gave him my best sad pleading look, pushing my brows up and together and pouting my lips, and I saw his deep brown eyes flash as he let out a shaky breath.

"Come on, Suranne, don't give me that look; it's seriously killing me," he muttered, running his hand through my hair softly.

"That's the idea," I sang teasingly as he released my hair and picked up the blanket from the ground. We walked over to his car; my hand in his and I glanced down, wondering how many girls he ever held hands with. I frowned at the thought of my being the only girl he'd ever opened himself up to. He couldn't have always been known as a womaniser.

"Have you ever actually been in a relationship?" I asked softly, looking back up at his face to gauge his reaction, expecting to see some clue as to what his answer would be.

He didn't disappoint.

Kane's face became clenched and dark. His whole body looked stiff and his movements seemed forced as we approached the passenger side of his car. He let go of my hand and kept it still by his side. Staying silent and avoiding eye contact, he opened the door, waiting for me to get in.

"Kane, wh—"

"Just get in the car, Suranne." He spoke slowly, his voice tight and distant. I cringed at the sudden coldness in his voice, slowly nodding my head as I got in. He shut the door softly and I clicked my belt, watching as he walked round to his side of the car. He seemed to be muttering to himself, his brows furrowed before he opened his door and got in, started the car, and peeled out of the car park.

As he drove, his fingers clenched the steering wheel and a tense silence hung between us. He kept his attention solely on the road and I kept my eyes glued to my lap, twirling my thumbs nervously and wondering what was so bad about his last relationship. Just before we pulled up to my aunt's he sighed and loosened his hold on the steering wheel. He parked in the drive and turned off the engine, the car becoming deathly quiet apart from our breathing. I kept my eyes on my lap but I could feel his stare on me even though he stayed quiet, watching me.

"Suranne," he murmured, and I flinched at the sudden sound of his voice after the silence that had occupied the car. I kept my eyes on my lap, not quite ready to look at his face.

"Suranne," he murmured again. "*Look at me.*"

I slowly lifted my head to look at him, and saw that his face had completely softened and no longer had its hard edge. His chocolate-brown eyes were shining with deep emotion and he gave a small smile in apology.

"I'm sorry, OK?" he said softly, reaching out to caress my cheek and I sighed and leaned into him, smiling absently at how touching him always made me feel at ease. He smiled back warmly, and leaned over to press his lips gently to mine. I wrapped an arm around his neck to keep him closer, causing him to groan and pull away.

"You should go, before I take you right here, right now," he said in his seductive low voice, his eyes shining dangerously as they raked over my body. I smiled sweetly at him.

"What if that's what I want, Kane?" I asked innocently, biting my lip and looking up at him, smirking as his eyes darkened and his fists clenched on his lap.

"I'll pick you up tomorrow." He jerked his head towards my door, a silent signal for me to get out of the car and I grinned at him, giving him a small chaste kiss on the lips and lingering there for a while. "See you tomorrow," I whispered against his mouth and he inhaled sharply.

I leaned back and smirked once more. Then I got out of the car, gave a small wave over my shoulder, opened my front door, and closed it behind me. I leaned against it and sighed, closing my eyes with a happy, dreamy grin on my face.

I wished that tomorrow would just come already.

## 20. RETURNING THE FAVOUR

### Suranne

My alarm clock buzzed that it was 7 a.m. I groaned and rolled over. As yesterday's events caught up with me I shot up, smiling sleepily to myself before pulling back the covers and padding to the bathroom to get ready.

Throughout the shower, teeth brushing, and hair fixing, my face retained its lazy, sleepy smile. My thoughts constantly revolved around Kane, and as I glanced quickly in the mirror, I did a double take.

I hardly recognised myself.

My eyes were bright and dancing wildly, my face was warm and flushed with a stupid grin still plastered on my face.

I was one hundred percent happy.

I applied a small amount of mascara and lip gloss, taking a final glance at my reflection before leaving the bathroom, grabbing my book bag, and heading downstairs. I walked into the kitchen and spotted a folded note on the kitchen table, my name written clearly on the front. Dropping my bag by the door and walking over to the table I grabbed the note and unfolded it. It was from my aunt.

*Had to leave early. Office is hectic this month. Probably won't be home till after 9:00. You're on your own for dinner.*

*Xxx*
*Aunt C*

107

My smile grew as I read the letter. I loved being home alone, and my aunt trusted me so much more than my mother had. I had more freedom. Freedom to watch, eat, and listen to whatever I wanted without anyone objecting. I had a feeling today was going to be a good day.

All of a sudden I heard a rap at the door, and jumped, startled by the noise. Then my excitement grew, knowing who would be on the other side. My mind ran through the possible alternatives on how he would look this morning.

Would his hair be neatly spiked up, or had he run his hand through it so many times it had become slightly messy, yet still held its attractiveness? Would he be wearing his light blue jeans, hung low and looking all seductive, or his dark navy-bordering-on-black ones, which he seemed to be favoring lately?

Either way, I knew he would look amazing and sexy. I practically ran to the door, picking up my bag on the way, and heaving it open, letting out a heavy breath as his sweet cologne assaulted my senses.

He certainly didn't disappoint.

His hair was indeed spiked neatly up at the front, begging my hands to run through it and make it that sexy dishevelled mess that I preferred. He was wearing his diamond stud in his ear, which I was doubly tempted to just nibble on. His warm brown eyes were bright, shining excitedly at me; his soft, full lips were turned up into a wide smile. His tanned skin was a blinding contrast to his crisp white button-down shirt, the first two buttons undone, revealing the top of his perfectly toned chest. His cuffs were rolled up his forearms and, as I had predicted, the dark navy jeans, fitting him perfectly and giving a tasty view of his arse when he walked.

He looked delicious.

"Hey," I breathed, my face beaming at him, and my wide grin still in place as he smiled back down at me.

"Hey," he murmured and I sighed in contentment, my ears becoming happily reacquainted with his smooth melodic tone. He leaned down and captured my lips with his own, kissing me softly. His sweet cologne put my mind in a dreamy haze and I ran my tongue along his juicy lower lip, biting it softly. He sighed into my mouth and cupped my face with his hand, wrapping his other arm tightly around me and pulling me closer to his body. Slipping his tongue between my lips he swirled it with mine tentatively, causing me to moan at the taste of him. I could taste the faint mint of his toothpaste mixed with a husky, salty but sweet taste, driving me insane.

He really was delicious.

I broke the kiss, panting for air, my chest heaving against his as his eyes burned into my own. His face slipped into an adorable pout and his brows were furrowed, confused as to why I'd stopped kissing him. I laughed at the hurt expression on his face, shaking my head at how cute he looked.

"As much as I would love to do nothing more than stand outside my front door and kiss you, we really do have to get going." I smiled at him, pecking him once more on the lips before breaking out of his grasp to walk to the car, but instead of releasing my arm, he pulled me tighter against him, ducking his head to whisper in my ear.

"I fucking missed you."

He dragged his nose along the base of my neck, inhaling slightly, and placed a wet open-mouthed kiss just below my ear. I let out a shaky breath, shuddering against him.

"I missed you, too," I murmured, turning my face to look him in the eye, not understanding the raw emotion I saw swirling in his chocolate eyes. He smiled warmly at me, before standing up straight, dropping his arm, and running his other hand through his hair quickly.

Yes . . . now he looked perfect.

He inclined his head towards the car and I nodded and shut the front door, locking it then following him, veering off to get in the passenger seat as he got in the driver's side. I clicked my belt and he started the engine and backed out, throwing his arm over the back of my seat and looking behind him instead of using his mirrors. Once he had successfully reversed from the drive, he smiled at me, realising I had been watching his face the entire time. He gave a quick, sexy wink then turned his attention back to the road.

I sighed and closed my eyes as we made our way to school, thinking back to how he'd kissed me at the door this morning. My lips involuntarily pulled up into a smile at the memory, and I felt warm fingers brushing against my cheek softly. I opened my eyes and locked them with Kane's.

"What are you smiling about?" he asked, flicking his eyes to the road and back to me.

I couldn't keep from blushing, knowing full well that he knew what I was thinking about. Then a thought suddenly came to me, and my face abruptly changed into one of worry, eyes wide, and my heart skipped a beat.

Kane noticed my change of mood and frowned at me, diverting his concentration from me to the road and back, repeatedly.

"What is it?" he asked seriously, his face contorted with concern.

"You're taking me to school," I breathed, my palms becoming sweaty as I glanced quickly out of the windshield. We would be there any moment and I turned back to him, my eyes even wider with worry.

Kane didn't seem to grasp what I was so worried about, and raised an eyebrow. "Yeah . . . So?"

"People will see!" I exclaimed, my breath quickening with nerves. I didn't know whether Kane wanted people to know about us, but it was pretty certain that when they saw me getting out of Kane's car, word would spread.

"I don't give a shit, Suranne. They can see or say whatever they goddamn want," he replied in a firm tone, his eyes flashing in anger before warming slightly. I took a deep breath and nodded slowly as he took my hand in his and squeezed it reassuringly.

"Don't worry about them, OK?" he murmured softly, raising his eyebrows daring me to disagree. I gave him a weak smile, nodding, and he flashed his cocky crooked grin at me as we pulled into the lot. I stared out the window towards a large group of students lounging around before the first bell sounded, staring at the car with their mouths slightly agape. Some were leaning in to murmur to their friends, causing them to turn as well and glance in our direction.

I stole a look at Kane, and he was the perfect picture of calm. His face was relaxed as he maneuvred gracefully into an empty space, seemingly unaware of all the eyes firmly locked on his car. He still had hold of my hand, and as he turned the engine off, he turned to me and stopped me from opening the door.

"Let me do that," he said softly, whilst he unbuckled his belt.

"Why?" I enquired. I was perfectly able to open my own door, and Kane doing it would draw even more attention to us. He raised an eyebrow and smirked at me.

"Can't I even open the door for my girl?" His voice sounded innocent, but his sexy smirk gave off something different altogether. I smiled warmly at the endearment, my stomach flipping at the thought of him actually calling me His Girl. I took a deep breath and nodded at him and he grinned, his bright chocolate eyes swirling with intense emotion. Then he opened his door and casually jogged over to my side.

I took a deep breath trying to calm my nerves as he opened the door and held out a hand. I eyed the hand warily, my eyes darting around me self-consciously before resting on Kane. His stare was reassuring, silently telling me that he was there for me, giving me the final push of strength that I needed to face what today was bound to bring.

I took his hand and he pulled me out of the car, shutting the door softly behind me. I smiled coyly up at him, refusing to concentrate on anything else but his face at the moment. My heart was hammering, my mind working overtime, reeling with the whispering and looks we were probably getting. I squinted my eyes closed, wishing that I could become as calm as Kane and will myself not to care about the others.

Suddenly I felt myself being pushed up against the car, Kane's sweet, mind-numbing scent filling my senses as he pressed against me, and I snapped my eyes open as they locked directly with a pair of burning, deep-brown ones.

"Trust me, Suranne," he whispered, and I was reminded of yesterday in the park, when I had said the exact same words to him, trying to reassure him that I wasn't going anywhere.

Now he was returning the favour.

He ducked his head and pressed his lips gently to mine. My ears registered a string of shocked gasps around us, as, for the first time, they saw Kane actually kissing someone on the lips.

My chest swelled with a pool of pride as I thought about how that Someone was me.

Kane had obviously realised this also, and pulled away from me, smirking yet breathing heavily. I grinned at him, a new sense of happiness spreading through my entire body.

"I trust you," I murmured back, and gripped his hand tightly knowing that, with him next to me, I would be able to face anything this day decided to throw at me . . .

## 21. REVELATIONS

### Kane

"I trust you," she murmured to me, and gripped my hand tightly, turning us slightly towards the school building but still keeping eye contact with me. I knew she was nervous as hell, but I had repeated the same words she had used on me yesterday, knowing that if she could heal me in ways I couldn't explain, then maybe I could do the same for her. It seemed to work.

I smirked back at her, brushed my thumb over the back of our intertwined fingers, and ran my other hand through my hair. I had styled it as usual this morning, but it always ended up all over the place by the end of the day. Before, I would get pissed about the habit I had, but Suranne had told me she liked it better, so I wasn't gonna complain.

I thought back to yesterday, and how, for the last three years, I'd felt like something was missing, and that I'd finally felt complete when she was there. But reality had smashed down on me like some huge rock as soon as I got home from our day at the park. I had walked in to find Ashley in the kitchen on her knees, sobbing and wiping her face, my eyes zeroed in on the small amount of blood that coated her fingers and the shards of glass scattered on the kitchen floor.

I ran up to her, not caring that I had left the front door wide open, and fell to the ground, gripping her shoulders tightly.

"Ashley, what's wrong?" I asked erratically, not really needing her to reply. I already knew the fucking answer.

She had lifted her face and stared at me with wide eyes holding a huge ocean of gut-wrenching pain. Too much for someone who was only twelve years old. I cursed myself for not being there, too busy smiling and feeling happy like a selfish dick while my little sister had to deal with the burden of our mother who was, at that moment, spewing her guts in the upstairs bathroom.

"When's it going to stop?" she breathed and her small, round and once-joyous face looked haggard and sad. Her eyes were red and puffy from crying and her face shone from the wet tears sliding down her cheeks.

I sighed heavily and wrapped my arms around her, pulling her to my chest and resting my chin on top of her little head, rocking us back and forth slowly.

"I'm sorry Ash, I'm so sorry. I wish I could fix it, believe me. I'm trying, OK? I need you to stay strong for me, I know you're already trying so hard, and you're doing great, trust me. But I need you to hang on just a little longer, OK?" I whispered, kissing her hair lightly as she sniffled and nodded weakly against my shirt.

I pulled away from her, inspecting her hands for any bits of glass as I grabbed a dishcloth and gently wiped away the blood. She winced slightly, her face turning into a grimace as I grabbed some disinfectant and dabbed it over the cuts.

"If this happens again, and I'm not here, call me, OK? Don't try and clean this shit up yourself, Ashley. You wait for me to get home and do it." I sighed, shaking my head and kissing her hands gently. She squirmed under my lips and I grinned at her, trying to lighten the mood. Her brown eyes glowed infinitesimally as she smiled back up at me, the sides of her eyes crinkling up like they always used to, before our mother had gone off the rails.

I nudged her arm playfully and told her to go upstairs and get cleaned up. Then I picked up the shattered remains of yet another glass and dumped it in the trash. That night I made a promise to myself that I was going to stay home after school and really try and sort this shit out before it got any worse. Which meant the mornings and school were the only times I would be able to be with Suranne, and I planned on savoring that as much as I could.

A gentle squeeze of my hand brought me back to the present and I looked over at Suranne. She was frowning up at me, her face etched with concern. I smiled weakly back at her, and squeezed her back, silently trying to tell her that I was alright. She smiled back at me, and I felt my breath hitch and my heart beat faster.

I'd never get over the effect she had on me.

I pulled my eyes away from her face and they widened as they met what was staring back at us. It seemed like the whole school had stopped what they were doing and were turned to us, their entire concentration fixed solely on our joined hands. I heard Suranne take a deep breath and I snapped my eyes back to her face. She was staring up at me all wide-eyed, looking like she was about to pass out.

I leaned in and kissed her temple lightly, trying to reassure her that it was OK, and gently tugged her hand towards the school building. It seemed to snap her back to the present and she smiled weakly up at me, following me as we slowly walked past the gaping idiots just standing, or rather, glaring at us both.

"Everyone's staring, Kane," she whispered to me, leaning her head close to my shoulder. I let go of her hand and wrapped my arm round her waist possessively, shrugging at her words, because I didn't particularly give a shit.

"Let them," I said simply as we reached the building and walked past the office. Even the receptionists were eyeing us curiously, and I glared at them, telling them with my eyes to mind their own damn business.

Suranne sighed and dropped her head on my shoulder as we walked. I held her more tightly against me, loving the sexy curve of her waist beneath my fingertips as that edible smell of her hair drifted up my nose.

She was too damn sexy for her own good.

As we reached the end of the hall and turned towards the end of the building, I spotted Lawrence with his back to us. He was with Jake and Devon, the two other guys who I usually practiced basketball with. Jake nudged Lawrence as soon as he spotted us and I could feel Suranne tense up slightly, which meant that she had noticed it, too, but by that time it was too late. Lawrence was already turning in our direction. I heard Suranne suck in a sharp breath and seemed to hold it there as his gaze lingered on the two of us, then narrowed when he looked down and saw my hand on her hip. As he continued glaring at it, his jaw clenched and his hands balled into fists.

Suranne suddenly planted her feet and stopped dead next to me. I looked down at her frowning, a panic surging through me thinking that she didn't want to be seen with me or some shit, and I subconsciously got angry. I had risked a lot more than she had by walking into this damn school after I'd just kissed her outside.

"What the hell are you doing?" I asked, glaring down at her. Her wide gray eyes snapped up to mine, widening in shock at the angry tone in my voice.

"I—I . . . This is my class," she stammered in a weak voice, her accent drawing out the word *class* in a way that sounded too hot for words.

I looked behind her, and spotted the class door that plainly said *English* in bold letters above it. I had been so focused on Lawrence that I hadn't even realized we had reached her class, and I had snapped at her for no goddamn reason.

I half groaned, half sighed, and ran my hand through my hair, smirking slightly when I noticed Suranne following the movement with parted lips. She loved that crap.

"Shit, yeah I'm sorry. I didn't realize," I mumbled, feeling like a jerk for having to apologize to her twice in the space of two days for acting like a complete dick. She smiled back at me reassuringly and nodded. I saw her eyes flicker to my lips before returning back to my eyes, a soft shade of longing in them, and I smiled warmly at her, knowing that regardless of where we were I wouldn't be able to deny this girl anything.

I leaned down, and noticed her eyes widen as she realized what I was about to do. She shifted nervously as my lips got closer to her own.

"Kane . . . really? Like, here?" she murmured, her eyes flitting nervously around her and I grinned, still ducking my head closer till our lips were an inch apart.

"Yes, here," I whispered, brushing my lips against hers softly and immediately feeling that jolt zing in my lips and tingle down in my chest, surprised that I got the same feeling each time I kissed her.

She sighed softly and parted her lips for me, moving them gently with my own, then I pulled away and grinned crookedly at her, winking and brushing the hair off her shoulder as she just looked at me, breathing heavily.

"I'm taking you home after school, so don't let me see you with Lawrence." I raised an eyebrow to make sure she understood. Her face twisted into a grimace at the mention of his name, and I could tell she was nodding at me reluctantly.

"Isn't he supposed to be your best friend?" she breathed gently.

"I don't care who he is. He's not gonna try and mess with my girl." I smirked, and saw her eyes gleam as I called her "my girl." With a soft chuckle I kissed her cheek, then walked away to get to my own damn class before my teacher got all pissy.

Classes seemed to drag throughout the day, and every time I sat down everyone seemed to be staring at me constantly. Was it so impossible for them to turn the hell around and carry on with their own life? And I was constantly thinking about how people were treating Suranne so that by the time lunch rolled around I was nearly jumping out of my seat to go see her, only to be ordered to practice by Coach Clapton. I couldn't concentrate on anything else but her, totally shocked at how much I actually missed her. I had never missed a girl so damn much.

Practice lasted till the end of the day and when he finally let us go to get changed, I sprinted back to the changing room, not even bothering with a shower, but just spraying extra deodorant on.

As I walked out to the lot, my chest became warm with the excitement of finally seeing her again, and just being us, without any further interruptions. As I neared my car, I spotted her, and subconsciously smiled.

The smile soon faded.

Suranne was having an argument, and as I got closer I could hear her voice quite clearly.

"What the hell has it got to do with you anyway? I don't understand what your problem is; he doesn't treat me like the rest of them!"

From my angle I couldn't see who she was arguing with, but whoever it was, I planned to put them in their place.

And then I heard her voice.

"Listen, you weren't *there*, OK? I saw what it was like for the girl who was with him like you are . . . It won't *last*." She sneered back at Suranne and I closed my eyes, really hoping that nothing more would be said.

I started walking faster, trying to reach them before shit got out of hand.

"And how the hell would you know anything about us? You haven't been there when it's just me and him, you haven't seen the side I have," I heard Suranne spit, and could just imagine how her face would be twisted in anger right now.

"Trust me, I know," I heard thrown back at her, and I knew what was coming next.

"*HOW?*" Suranne exclaimed, throwing her hands up in exasperation. "How could you possibly know *SHIT?* You keep going on about this girl who used to be with him, but how do you know anything about her?!"

And just like that, I knew this was bad. I closed my eyes, waiting for the inevitable as the parking lot became coated in silence and I heard the unmistakeable sound of Suranne's opposition take a deep breath, before she spoke.

"Because I was that girl . . ."

I groaned and dropped my head, shaking it angrily at her words.

If I didn't already hate Kate before she dragged out all our fucking history in the school parking lot, then I definitely did now.

## 22. THE STORM APPROACHES

### Suranne

I nearly heaved, my chest dropping in my stomach with a large thud. I heard a familiar groan behind me and whipped my body around, glaring at Kane, who seemed to be avoiding eye contact at all costs.

But that wasn't going to work.

"Kane?" I said coolly, my voice acidic even to my own ears as he cringed at the unfamiliar tone, his eyes lingering on the pavement.

"Why didn't you tell me?" I murmured gently. All of a sudden, these past few weeks started to make sense, the slight tension between the two of them. That day in the canteen when Kane grabbed a chair and sat next to Lawrence instead of the free seat next to Kate. The way he never conversed with her, and avoided even *acknowledging* her existence. The way Kate regarded him, always seeming to hate him more than anyone else.

I thought back to my first day, when Kate had been at my locker and Kane had come up behind her. Now it all made sense. Why she had been so shocked when he spoke to her. I was guessing that had probably been the first time he had acknowledged her presence in who knows how long. Even if it was just to tell her to move.

I mentally slapped myself for not realising it before. Now that I knew, it was so blindingly obvious.

Kane came closer and touched my arm, trying to tug me away towards his car, away from the crowd that was now surrounding us, silently whispering to each other about my newly discovered information.

"Suranne, let's just . . . go, I'll explain everything," I heard him say softly. But before I could respond, Kate snorted and sneered at him.

"You know you're only gonna use her, then push her away like you did me, so what's the point?" she spat, before focusing back on me and touching my other arm softly. "Come on Suranne, you can come back to my house and we'll talk about it." She smiled pleadingly at me, and jerked her head towards her car, but Kane stepped forward, his fists clenched in anger.

"Piss off, Kate," he spat. "We don't need your nosy ass try'n'a screw up everything for me *AGAIN*, so why don't you just take your ass home and mind your own damn business?"

I just stood dumbfounded at the exchange I was witnessing between the two of them, their words confusing me even more.

"Screw you!" she screamed back at him, before waving for me to follow her. But Kane gripped my hand and halted my movements.

"Screw me?! . . . Nah, Kate. Not a chance," he responded bitterly. "You can try pulling your innocent wide-eyed bullshit, with your two-faced smile but that shit ain't gonna work with me." He looked down at me, his chocolate-brown eyes pleading. "Come on, Suranne. Let me take you home, OK?"

"What shit?!" I heard her exclaim, and as I looked back at her, I could see her eyes misting over, the tears threatening to spill down her cheeks. "I *loved* you, Kane."

124

I felt a pang of guilt at the pain that was laced in her words, and the twisted expression on her face. Once again she looked back at me, her wide green eyes still pleading with me to go with her as a lone tear slid down her cheek, but Kane just laughed bitterly from beside me, and shook his head slightly.

"Like hell you did. If you loved me, you wouldn't have been at my damn door that night throwing every-fucking-thing back in my face."

I felt dizzy as my head bounced back and forth between the both of them. I held up my hand, stopping Kate from replying, which probably would have kept us there all bloody night.

"Enough," I announced firmly. It was bad enough to find out that Kate had in fact, been the last person Kane had been in a proper relationship with. And now, standing here catching glimpses of what had happened, and their feelings towards each other, I seriously just needed to get out of there. But I was being pulled in two different directions.

"Just let me go with her, Kane. Nothing's going to change how I feel about you." I sighed dejectedly, and released my hand from Kane's firm grip.

"What?!" he blurted out at me, looking down, his brows furrowed in confusion.

I sighed again, and turned to him fully, looking him firmly in the eyes.

"I'll be fine, and I'll come see you straight after, OK? I promise," I murmured softly.

His eyes flashed with rejection slightly before they became startlingly blank, and dead looking. His face contorted in pain but he swallowed heavily, abruptly transforming it into a stiff, calm mask, expressing nothing. Just like his eyes.

He shrugged coldly at me, and no longer looked at me, gazing unseeingly at the parking lot behind me instead.

"Don't bother; I won't be able to see you later. I have to deal with stuff at home." His voice was cold and dismissive as he woodenly brushed past me without another word and got into his car, disappearing out of the lot almost instantly. I stared after him in shock. I had never seen someone whose emotions changed so quickly. He was worse than any PMSing girl.

I exhaled a breath irritably and turned back to Kate who had an apologetic look on her face, and a sad smile on her lips.

"This had better be good, Kate, because for some reason, I have a feeling Kane isn't too happy with me right now."

She sighed and nodded, leading me to her car.

***

"We were fourteen when we first got together." Kate's lips turned upwards slightly as she spoke, smiling at some distant memory.

"He was just as good looking." She laughed slightly, but the sound wasn't light, it was strained, tight and laced with unspoken pain. My first reaction was to feel smug that they were no longer together. But Kate had been one of my first friends here and her pain seemed to ignite something within me, and all I wanted to do was pull her into a hug.

I refrained however, and just sat stiffly, missing Kane's presence already. My body twisted in guilt, my mind flashed with images of his face becoming that cold mask, his eyes that frosty glass.

"He was just as popular, maybe not on the scale he is now with all the bitches, but we were like . . . the "it" couple." She sighed, and leaned her head in her hands.

"So, what? Did he cheat on you?" I asked skeptically and Kate's head snapped up, her teary eyes locking with mine as she shook her head quickly.

"No! . . . No, he was . . ." she tilted her head, her brows puckering as she thought of how to start her sentence.

"He was . . . perfect," she finally murmured. "He pretty much treated me like a damn princess, always telling me he loved me. And even though we were fourteen, I believed I loved him, too. I know I did," she insisted, her voice firm as her blonde waves fluttered over her shoulder gently.

"I loved the attention I got from being his girlfriend, and he loved seeing me happy. We hardly ever argued, he was so different from the guy he is now. He only swore on occasion when we were together," she whispered gently as her eyes gleamed vacantly.

"So what was the problem?" I snapped. The perfect 'happy couple' image she was burning into my skull was eating away at my envious mind, and, as selfish as it sounded, I wanted to hear about the destruction of their relationship. Not the happy times.

Her face seemed to flash in understanding, and she sighed wearily as her eyes once again filled with that heavily pained look as she took herself back to when they had split up.

"It was just after three years ago. We had been together seven months at the time," she finally spoke after a bout of silence. Her voice had become cold and distant, in contrast with the soft curvature of her face.

"Kane had been absent from school for a while . . . like two or three consecutive weeks. We all knew why. But during that time he hardly spoke to me. I think like once over the phone, and even that conversation was short. He just said he would ring me back. He never did."

I frowned as I thought about what would have been happening in his life three years ago that would have caused him to act like that all of a sudden. As cocky and laidback as Kane seemed, I knew he took things like his education seriously, so him not going to school sounded strange even to me.

Like a stinging slap in the face the answer struck me, and I gasped out loud as I understood the situation more fully.

Three years ago.

That was when his father had died.

Kate's detached voice shocked me from my stupor and I refocused on her words as they filled the space between us.

"He was distant when he did finally return to school, always . . . pushing me away." Her voice had become thick with emotion, and I saw her intake a deep breath as she pushed her emotions back.

"He was always snapping, sometimes going as far as just flat out telling me to 'fuck off and leave him alone' or just giving me the silent treatment."

I winced at her words, having never seen the full wrath of Kane's anger. But I certainly had witnessed glimpses of his frustration, and just from those I knew he could be nasty when he wanted to be.

She sighed heavily and finally locked her eyes with mine. They seemed guilty, almost desperate.

"I became tired of his ways, Suranne, but then . . . I knew about the plane crash, and I was sorry, I really was. I gave him time, comfort, all of my love, but . . . none of it . . . worked." Her voice was no longer detached, but full of insistence as if she was vowing what she was saying was the truth.

"I felt helpless; he only got worse, his nasty words increasing. He was always swearing, getting into fights, cussing at something and at first, I just . . . breathed deep and accepted. Because I knew he was in pain, Suranne, but I felt as if he . . . I dunno. *Hated me.*"

I sighed and finally relented, putting my arm around her shoulder. In truth, from what I had heard, none of it had been her fault. But neither was any of it Kane's. He was in unimaginable pain, and Kate just seemed to get stuck in the crossfire.

"One night I went to his house and when he came to the door, he looked tired, angry, and his eyes were red and puffy as usual. That was how he always looked." She murmured next to me as she leaned into my embrace, her soft blonde locks brushing against my neck.

"'What now? Wasn't I just on the phone with you?' is what he asked as soon as he saw me, but it was nothing new." She sighed.

"I told him I needed to speak to him but he just said 'Yeah, well, I don't have time to talk to you right now, Kate, didn't I say that already?'" Kate shook her head slightly and I grimaced, visualising how Kane would have looked that evening. But I stayed silent, allowing her to carry on.

"I told him I had had enough. I told him how I had tried to help him, giving him everything I could, and that I couldn't do it anymore." She sniffled and my arm became stiff around her shoulder as I realised with perfect clarity what she was telling me.

She had left him.

She had left him when he had needed her the most.

Now it all made sense and I internally kicked myself for deciding to go with Kate in the first place. I should have listened to Kane and let him tell me instead. I had promised him on the bench when he was upset and revealing his painful memory to me that I would never leave. That I would always be there, and yet, today I chose Kate over him. The same girl who, as I had just done, left him and walked away from his insecurities.

Kate carried on speaking but her words were no longer registering in my mind. All I knew was that I needed to go to Kane now. I had already been away from him for too long.

I quickly stood up from her bed and gathered my things together. Kate asked me what was wrong but I ignored her and put my book bag over my shoulder.

"I need you to write down Kane's address with simple directions on how to get there, Kate," I replied whilst rooting around in my bag for my phone.

"But . . . I don't understand," she stammered weakly and I sighed in frustration.

"Please, Kate, I just need it, OK?" I muttered dryly, desperately seeking out my phone so I could ring him. When I sensed no movement from Kate I began to get irritated and snapped my eyes up to hers.

"Please!" I snarled, and she jerked back from my voice before grabbing a slip of paper and pen from her drawer, writing his address down as quickly as her trembling fingers would allow, her occasional sniffles occupying the tense space between us. I breathed a sigh of relief as I caught a glimpse of the small silver phone in my bag and grabbed it, and dialed Kane's number, silently praying that he would pick up.

"Yeah, I'm too busy right now to pick up, but leave a message and I'll try and get back to ya bitches!"

I gritted my teeth at his voicemail message, making a personal note to remind him to change that once I got hold of him, but for now I was settling on him just picking up the bloody phone.

I dialed two more times only to be met with the same stupid message, and I growled in frustration, snapping the phone shut and snatching the address from Kate's nimble fingers as she looked at me, her eyes pleading and regretful.

I didn't sympathise with her now, and barely glanced back as I opened her bedroom door and retreated out of her house altogether. I needed to get to Kane and began quickly walking where she had directed, continuingly dialing Kane's number but still only getting his voicemail. After a while, I became worried. His twisted face, and rejected eyes filled my mind, and burned behind my eyelids. The guilt washed over me in waves and I started running, panting heavily as I got closer to his house praying that he would be home, to let me explain how sorry I was. Let me promise once again that I wasn't going anywhere and that I wanted to be with him.

As I rounded the last corner, I felt the tears stinging my eyes along with the wind and I pushed my limbs to move faster. I wanted to feel his pain, wanted to share it so that he didn't have to carry it all.

In my mind I chanted over and over, praying that I wasn't too late, and that he would still let me.

# 23. THE POISON AND THE ANTIDOTE

## Kane

Thanks to Kate, I couldn't help remembering that messed up day. I had heard the doorbell ring, and glanced at it blankly . . . staring unseeingly, not even curious as to whom it was. I knew my mother was upstairs, lost in another bottle, and thankfully, Ashley was hanging around her friends. I trudged to the front door and opened it, my eyes flashing with irritation at the figure in front of me.

"Wasn't I just on the phone with you?" I knew my voice was cold and acidic but I just didn't have the energy to care. Kate narrowed her eyes at me infinitesimally and I noticed there was a slight determination in her stare, but my mind just shrugged it off.

"I needed to talk to you," she spoke calmly and it pissed me off all the more having to listen to her voice that was so soft and calm while I was stuck here in this life of heartwrenching pain.

"Yeah, well, I don't have time to talk to you right now, Kate. Didn't I say that already?" I snapped at her, beyond irritated at how she never seemed to listen these days. I saw her eyes flash and her fists clench, and I should've known then that I had probably pushed it too much.

"I give up!" she exclaimed, throwing her hands in the air out of exasperation, her voice high and her eyes burning in anger. "I can't win! I give you support, space, time, comfort, and yet you still treat me like a piece of crap." She took a deep breath, and her wide green eyes became soft and regretful.

133

"I know you lost your dad, Kane, and I'm sorry, OK? I'm sorry, but you can't take your shit out on other people."

I just stood blinking at her. Of course I knew that, but right then, I couldn't deal with her, and yet, as bad as it sounded, I still wanted her near me. All I wanted to do was have her arm around me, but I didn't want her to think I was fucking weak. I was supposed to be the guy supporting her, not the other way around, and I needed time to support myself first, and even though it may have looked as though I didn't appreciate all the shit she was doing, I really did. It helped me. Not as much as I would have liked, but it helped all the same.

With these thoughts running through my mind, I'd stayed silent, frowning and leaning against the doorframe. Kate had obviously been waiting for an answer but I just looked at her. She sighed heavily and shook her head.

"I'm out Kane. I'm sorry." Her clear green eyes gave me one last look before she began to turn away, but then her words finally registered in my mind.

She was leaving me, giving up.

This realization snapped my mind back into focus, and these past few weeks came flashing to my mind. The distantness, the constant snapping at her, the pushing her away, never ringing her back. I reached out and grabbed her arm, to stop her from walking away. I needed her more than I wanted to let on, but I just expected her to understand and stick it out with me.

"No, Kate, I'm sorry please . . . I . . . I need you . . . My mom . . . She's . . . Shit," I muttered, stressing at the fact that I just couldn't spit it out. Why couldn't I just tell her I needed her help, that I was feeling so alone, with no one to turn to?

"Just, please Kate, give me another chance and I'll let you in," I pleaded, not caring if I sounded like a weak pussy . . . I wanted her to understand, I didn't want to lose her. She was the only person I had.

"I need you, Kate." I choked, praying that the tears didn't come, that she would stay, that I could open up to her and give her everything I had rather than pushing her away, hoping that I would still be able to love her through all this shit.

Hoping that she would love me back.

My whole world fell when a tear escaped her eye and slid down her cheek as she shook her head.

No. She was shaking her head at me? She couldn't.

"I'm sorry, Kane. I can't. It's not fair to me," she sniffled, the wind blowing against her hair, causing it to wind around her face and lash wildly about in the darkness. She gazed back at me, her eyes glassy with tears. "You'll only push me away," she whispered into the dead space between us. I just stood, unable to comprehend the fact that she was still shaking her head. My chest tightened painfully as everything came back at me. I felt like I was hanging off the edge of a very high building, and everything with my father dying, my mom turning to a bottle of alcohol, and the stress of school bitching about my absence were like kicks to my fingers clinging to the edge. Kate had been the only one holding my hand, keeping me there, balanced on the thin line.

But now?

Now she had just kicked me herself, and I fell. I felt the anger and hatred seep through my heart, into the blood pumping through my veins, and out through every single pore of my body. I felt the resentment burn in my eyes as I glared at her, my body going icy cold as she continued staring at me, sniffling and wiping her eyes with the back of her hand, as if I had been the one to break her heart.

"Fine," I snapped, clenching my fists to try and reign in my poisonous anger. "Fuck you," I spat at her, gritting my teeth. "Get the hell off my property and don't so much as ever look at me!" I slammed the door, the vibrations reverberating through the house. I drew my arm back and punched the door angrily with my fist, the pain shooting up my arm as my knuckles connected with the solid wood. But I just carried on punching it, again and again and again till I felt those bitch traitor tears easing down my cheeks and dripping onto my cradled fist, burning through the skin as the salty substance stung the bleeding cuts over my knuckles.

***

"Damn," I muttered as I came back to the present, the same slicing pain I'd felt that night tightening in my chest, except it was a hell of a lot worse. I had opened up to Suranne, told her everything. She had let me reach back up to the edge of that goddamn building and then she had helped pull me back to safety, away from the darkness, away from feeling like I had the weight of the world on my shoulders, she had let me shrug off everything when I was with her, and now where the hell was she?

With *Kate.*

I laughed darkly to myself at the irony of the moment. Trust this mess to come back and bite me in the ass just when I catch a glimpse of damn happiness, for the first time in three long, painful, lonely years. Three years full of me banging a different chick every night, sometimes more than one depending on my mood. Three years of going to parties, drinking like a fish, and getting high whenever I got the chance.

And yet it was the worst three years of my life.

I glanced down at my hands, tracing the scars from that night that were still jaggedly ingrained into the skin over my knuckles. A reminder of the anger, the hurt, and the betrayal I'd felt, and continued to feel, until I had met Suranne.

And now she was gone.

I threw my head back, slamming it hard against the head-board of my bed, wincing as the pain shot through me, but I didn't care, the physical pain was much easier to stand than the aching, burning pain I felt constricting in my chest. Every breath was strained and labored and I shook my head, squinting my eyes tightly shut, willing it to go away. But closing my eyes had been a mistake.

A big misake.

Instantly she was there, her soft face and wide gray eyes shining back at me. A full smile graced her rosy lips and her long, mahogany hair glided past her shoulders and bounced smoothly against the air sweeping around her.

That vision was the last straw. The pain in my chest reared, its long talons reaching out and wrapping around my very being, consuming me, sucking me back into the darkness, and as much as I tried, it was too strong to fight. So I let it, I let it pull me back, but kept my eyes closed, not wanting to lose the image of her face. Her beautiful, smiling face, and then her voice sang out to me . . .

"Kane!"

I felt my lips turn up into a smile as the pain receded slightly upon hearing her voice, and I begged it to never stop, hoped it would anchor me through whatever the hell was going on with me at the moment.

"Kane! Open the damn door!"

My eyes snapped open and I was shocked to see my bedroom encased in darkness. I had been holed up in here without even noticing that it was now evening. Someone was pounding on the downstairs door and I snapped my head in the direction of my bedroom door. I forced myself up, walked over, and opened it slightly, peering down the stairs.

"Kane!"

It was her.

I flew down the stairs and wrenched back the door and my breath left me as my eyes met hers.

Her hair was wild, sticking out and whipping furiously against the wind, her deep gray eyes were wide, and burning into mine with an intensity I had never encountered before as she launched herself into my arms.

"Oh, Kane . . . Kane, I'm so sorry," she sobbed into my shoulder as I wrapped my arms tightly around her, crushing her against my chest and gulping down her scent, each breath of her healing me, like she was the antidote to some noxious shitty infection that had been living within me. Her warmth burned through my arms and spread throughout my limbs. The familiar tingles I got whenever I touched her assaulted my skin and I pulled back, lifting her face and cupping it firmly in my hands. Looking down at her, trapped in her gaze, I leaned down and brushed my lips against hers, shivering at the feel, the taste . . . at her.

She wrapped her arms around my neck and snaked her hands into my hair at the nape of my neck, tilting her head and deepening the kiss as our lips moved feverishly against each other, desperate to get closer but not sure how to.

It was then that I knew I loved her . . . She wasn't at my door, crying and sniffling shaking her head saying she couldn't do it anymore like some fucking coward.

She was at my door, crying and sniffling, wrapping her arms around me and telling me with her kiss that she was willing to have me for who I was.

She understood me . . . and I loved her for that shit . . .

## 24. UNSPOKEN WORDS OF LOVE

### Suranne

Kane carried on kissing me, our mouths moving against each other heatedly. Kane moved his tongue gently against mine and I shivered in his arms. As he hummed against my lips, the kisses transformed into slow, soft and gentle pecks. I opened my eyes and found his closed, his forehead no longer wrinkled with that crease of pain that I had seen when he swung open the door. When he opened his eyes, they were red and puffy, his hair in wild disarray.

"Suranne," he whispered against my lips. He sighed softly before kissing my mouth again, cupping my face gently in his hands, brushing my cheeks, and winding his hand in my hair. Our breathing became panting, and he pulled away for oxygen, resting his forehead against mine. Our lips barely touched and our breaths bounced against each other's.

"You came," he murmured gently. His full red lips twitched into a small smile, then disappeared almost as quickly. His eyes flashed with worry. "How much did she tell you?" he asked hoarsely, pulling away. I stood, blinking at him, stunned by his sudden change in behaviour, but I stepped forward and grasped his hands firmly in mine, locking my gaze on his deep chocolate-brown eyes.

"I don't care about what she said, Kane. She's not important to us." I raised an eyebrow, waiting for confirmation about the last part. He nodded slowly and I sighed in relief as he pulled me close once more, pressing a soft kiss against my hair then resting his head atop of mine.

"Where's your family?" I mumbled into his chest, feeling it vibrate with his humourless chuckle before his smooth voice rang against my ears.

"Who knows where my mom is. Probably on the streets, buying as much alcohol as possible and consuming it all before she gets back, knowing I'd take it from her and throw it the hell away."

I hugged him more tightly and wondered how he and his sister managed. I didn't know much about Ashley, he only mentioned her briefly yesterday at the park when he was telling me about his father's plane crash.

"Ashley's at her friend's. She tends to stay away more these days. I don't blame her." He sighed wearily, and I pressed a kiss against his shirt-covered skin, then looked up, propping my chin against his firm chest. His arms wrapped more tightly around my waist.

"It's not your fault, Kane. You're only seventeen; you can't be expected to handle everything." His face warmed as he looked down at me, his swirling brown eyes melting my concentration, burning intensely into my own. Ducking his head, he pressed his soft lips to mine lightly, lingering there for a second before pulling away. His expression changed into one of anticipation and excited eagerness; his eyes burned brightly with some new idea.

"Come on, I wanna show you something." He grinned briefly and grasped my hand and pulled me into the direction of the stairs. I quickly craned my head to look around his house, shocked that I hadn't realised how beautiful it was. The furniture was all soft chocolate and cream colours, and the kitchen countertops were a shiny, sleek black between modern appliances. "You have a nice home," I muttered as he hastily pulled me up the stairs. He chuckled and thanked me briefly as we approached a door which I assumed led to his room. He pushed it open and dragged me in, not letting go until we were planted in the middle. My eyes widened as I took in his personal space. A large king-sized bed was pressed up against the eastern wall with sheets, from what I could make out, of black silk. A flat-screen TV was attached to the western wall facing his bed. He stood beside me smirking, watching my reaction as my eyes travelled around the room. He ducked his head to whisper softly in my ear.

"Turn around, baby."

I shivered as his words sent tingles down my spine and heard him breathe a quiet laugh at my reaction. I slowly turned, taking a deep breath in preparation for whatever it was that he wanted to show me. When my eyes finally met the object in the corner of the room, partially hidden behind his door, I gasped loudly and covered my mouth.

"Kane . . ." I whispered, too numb to move. A beautiful, sleek Baldwin R1 medium-sized grand piano stared back at me, the inner lining of bright gold merging with the shiny black exterior. The mahogany slide covered the keys and my whole being ached to push it up.

"I know," he murmured softly into the silent air surrounding us, and then he once again took my hand and brought me over to the extraordinary instrument, pulling out the leather bench and sitting down, patting the space next to him. I tentatively sat next to him, silently waiting for him to lift the sliding cover. I released a shaky breath when he did, and the startlingly white keys screamed back at me, contrasting with the smaller black keys between them, begging to be played.

"May I?" I asked softly, reaching my hand out, waiting for his approval.

"Of course."

I smoothly stroked the keys, relishing the cool ivory through my warm fingertips, and gently played an A chord. My eyes closed as the melancholy sound ricocheted against the walls of Kane's room. I opened them and situated my fingers, starting to gently play the right hand of Yiruma's *River Flows in You*. I wasn't able to reach the left-hand keys with Kane next to me, but enjoyed the tinkling sound all the same. Kane quickly lifted his left hand and added the accompaniment as I carried on playing through the first couple of bars. I smiled at him as we continued playing the gentle tune together, though I sometimes missed a key when my eyes focused on Kane's long, slender fingers moving with a grace I had never attained. He would smirk arrogantly, and I would blush, knowing that he had caught me looking. I sighed as we finished the song, Kane shifting to play the last chord, letting it ring out and shimmer against our ears.

"You play well, mostly," he chuckled, and pressed a gentle kiss to my cheek.

"Thanks . . . so do you." He then graced me with his sexy, crooked grin, his eyes bright with warm emotion as he gazed back at me. His lips parted, and he sucked in a quick breath "Suranne . . . I . . ." he trailed off, his eyes burning down into mine, trapping me in his stare, and I felt paralysed.

"You what?" I breathed, my heart flipping in my chest and my breathing becoming heavier as the intensity of his stare evoked in the pit of my stomach an uncontrollable burning desire I had never felt before. It spread through me, mainly occupying my heart, but expanding slowly through my veins with every beat.

Kane broke eye contact and sighed, running his hand through his hair and gripping it tightly, muttering to himself too quietly for me to hear. I could only distinguish a few words.

"... her ... too much ... just say it ... shit."

I grinned at his adorable discomfort and placed a gentle hand on his face, curving it to fit perfectly against his cheek. He brought his attention back to me, and I immediately saw the tension dissipate from his features. Whatever it was that he wanted to tell me, it seemed to have been forgotten for the moment.

He leaned towards me and brought his lips within an inch of mine, obliterating my senses. I could almost taste his lips as they turned up into a small smile.

"Let me play something for you . . ." he whispered, pressing his lips gently against mine, parting them minutely and running the tip of his tongue against my lower lip. The sensation of his wet tongue caused me to shiver and breathe a light moan. He pulled away and winked at me, turning back to the piano, his hands hovering over the keys. He lowered them and pressed gently, and I recognised the song straight away. I smiled broadly as his fingers continued gliding swiftly over the keys. He bowed his head in concentration as the delicately sweet notes of *Kiss the Rain* filtered through the air.

He looked down at me briefly, and I saw his eyes laced with a hint of sadness, or disappointment, and I frowned, trying to guess the reason he would be sad. His hands continued to sweep over the keys, the beautiful music filling the room as his eyes continued to burn into mine.

"Listen, Suranne," he murmured, his voice strained.

"I am," I replied softly, smiling as the song reached the bridge and his hands went further down the keys to play the chords an octave lower. He shook his head lightly, and his eyes flicked back to the piano slightly, then back to me.

"No, Suranne. Listen."

I closed my eyes and let my body open up to the music as Kane pressed more heavily on the chords, the deep bass bleeding through the room and vibrating in every fibre of my body as if communicating some underlying message. As he weaved back through the first half, the light notes tinkled against my ears, wrapping around me, consuming me. All I could hear, and all I was, in that moment was the music. I felt emotion swell through me, so strong and intense that it knocked me breathless. Is *this* what Kane had meant when he told me to listen? Is this what he wanted me to feel? This. . . Love?

*His* love?

I gasped and snapped my eyes open, only to be met with the most intense pair of brown eyes imaginable. Kane had never stared at me like this, and his playing faltered, lacing the room with eerie silence as he continued to gaze at me, the bright chocolate of his eyes swirling and burning ferociously into mine. My skin burst into flames and my breathing hitched as my heart began to pump a burning desire through my veins.

"Kane," I whispered, my skin blazing under his stare as his eyes dragged over my body, his chest rising heavily, and his tongue sweeping lazily over his lower lip. His gaze fluttered from my eyes, to my lips, to my hair, to my neck before going back over my body. I shivered and closed my eyes as my breathing became heavier and my desire to have him touch me increased tenfold.

"Suranne." His hoarse voice assaulted my ears and I slowly met his gaze, gasping once again as his eyes stared back at mine, his hair even messier in that sexy, unruly way. I couldn't handle the space between us for much longer.

"Get over here," I murmured, and his lips smashed against my own before I could finish my sentence. I fisted my hands in his hair, gripping tightly as our mouths attacked each other. He groaned and slid his hands over my ribs, down my waist, and gripped my hips firmly. This unrecognisable, untameable feeling I felt coursing through me only increased with every movement of his lips against my own, and all of a sudden all I could think in my head was more.

*More, more, more.*

"More," I panted. He pulled away from my lips, his own breathing laboured as he peppered kisses along my neck. I tilted my head to give him better access, sighing at the sensation of his lips against my skin. The familiar tingles shooting through every bit of skin his lips touched and the thirsty raging desire I felt within me were becoming too much to handle.

I whimpered and gripped his hair more tightly. "*More,*" I pleaded. He lifted me off the bench, and I instinctively wrapped my legs around his waist. It was evident that he wanted more just as much as I did. He pushed his lips back against my own as he blindly shuffled towards his bed and our tongues swirled deliciously. After a few seconds we dropped, Kane falling on top of me, my desire still raging through my veins and I grabbed his shirt, ripping it open; the sound of his buttons bouncing off the floor echoed against the walls.

He broke the kiss and chuckled lightly, panting for air and pulling away to undo his belt buckle. He dropped his jeans and launched himself back at me, his hands roaming over my chest and torso. I sucked his lower lip between my teeth and bit down causing him to groan loudly and curse as he fumbled with my sweater before he yanked it over my head and tossed it across the room.

Our loud breathing filled the room as he pulled off my jeans and discarded my bra so it joined my sweater on his bedroom floor.

"Suranne," he moaned, trailing his eyes, black with lust, over my body. He lowered himself on top of me and stroked my face softly, his eyes dark and burning, but not just with want. There was something else, something stronger and intensifying as he carried on focusing on my face.

"You're beautiful," he muttered and dipped his head to brush his lips softly against mine, before trailing them to my cheek, across my jaw, and down my neck. His lips left a burning trail against my skin as he carried on his journey downwards.

After a moment, he sat back and I ran my hand down his chest, fingering the firm muscles of his abdomen and watching them twitch under my touch as he released a shaky breath.

I became nervous from his intense stare, and self-consciously attempted to close my legs, but his hands firmly gripped them, stopping my actions.

"Don't . . . don't hide from me, Suranne." His hoarse voice caused me to close my eyes and shiver.

His eyes quickly darted to his bedside table's drawer where he pulled out protection. Then, bending forward, he kissed me sweetly, his tongue sweeping across my lips. He carried on kissing me gently, but my desire for him was too strong, and my head was once again filled with that one-word chant.

*More, more, more.*

He seemed to get the message, massaging my knees with his hands before situating himself against me. I held my breath and closed my eyes, preparing for the sense of being filled, of being completed.

But there was nothing.

I opened my eyes and found Kane staring at me, his face masked in worry, his eyes seeming desperate.

"What's wrong?" I asked breathlessly.

"I'm afraid, Suranne," he choked, his voice tight.

I ran my hand up his arm, across his shoulders and back down his chest. "Afraid of what?" I asked softly.

"I don't *want* it to be the same. I *really* don't want it to be like the others." He breathed, his face screwing up even more, and his eyes becoming glassy with worry. I frowned at him, tilting my head in confusion. He sighed and dropped his head.

"The other chicks were meaningless. A distraction. Once I was done, I left," he murmured gently. Then his head lifted, and his eyes locked with my own, flaring with emotion as he continued to speak.

"I don't want *that* with you. I want more, I don't want it to feel like it did with them. Christ, I'm so damn nervous." He exhaled shakily and ran a hand through his hair. When I grabbed his hand he looked at me, his brows woven together in confusion.

"Kane, I've never felt like this. *Ever*. The feelings I have are just . . ." I sighed and shook my head, lost for words. "I can't tell you it will be different, Kane, but just trust what you feel."

He blinked at me for a while before lowering himself over me, kissing my lips roughly. I moaned at the change in his behaviour and pulled away panting for air.

"You're so sexy right now," he whispered and leaned back, positioning himself over me once again, his eyes focused back on my face, and I smiled back at him reassuringly. He gave a small smile as I felt him, and he sucked in a sharp breath, snapping his eyes shut.

My nerves spiked as he remained silent, and I pleaded for it not to be the same for him. Just as I was about to say his name, he let out the sexiest groan, and when he opened his eyes, they were bright with shock and elation.

I let out the breath I had been holding and smiled back at him, willing him to move. When I did, his eyes closed again and his head lowered, kissing me softly as he continued. His heavy breathing washed over my face when he parted, only to kiss me again.

The pleasure began to rise in me, reaching a new level, and as the sounds of our heavy breathing bounced off the walls, I felt a burning warmth approaching, threatening to spill and overtake my body. My nerve endings were frayed, alive with electricity.

His eyes opened and focused on mine and the burning fire in his stare finally pushed me over the edge. I closed my eyes tightly as I called out his name, eliciting a low groan from him as he shuddered and collapsed on top of me.

We lay quiet and numb. He took my hand and laced his fingers through mine.

"Well?" I asked breathlessly as I lazily turned to face him, "was it the same?"

He closed his eyes and his lips turned into a cocky smirk as his chest continued heaving from his heavy panting.

"Hell no. That was *heaven* . . ."

## 25. IMPOSSIBLE SPEECH

### Kane

I couldn't say it. It was like every time I tried, my throat would close up, not letting those three words escape from the furthest depths of my soul. I had wanted to tell her when I first opened the door that evening. I wanted to tell her when we were sitting at the piano. I wanted to tell her before I covered her, and let her consume me.

But I couldn't. And I had no idea why.

And yet I knew it wasn't because I didn't truly feel it. I loved her, I could tell every time I looked at her, every time I kissed those damn lips, every time my hands ghosted over her smooth skin, and every time her silvery gray eyes locked with my own. It tugged at my insides and twisted beautifully inside me sharper than a damn razor. Internally I screamed it. Every second I spent with her, every time her light laugh rang in my ears. Every time I heard her lips part allowing a moan to escape and swirl in the air, flying around my very being.

But I couldn't tell her.

It had been two weeks since she had shown up at my front door. Afterwards we had just stayed in my bed. I was still overwhelmed at how different she felt to me, and how completely taken I had become with her. Being with her was the best thing in this universe, and I reminded her every damn day.

And now, two weeks later my life had started to gain some light. A light which I was holding onto for dear life, clinging to its thin thread, begging not to slip and float back into the darkness. I had tried persuading my mom to go to AA meetings and sort herself the hell out. Of course she had rejected the idea, and every day I gave her other options, finally pulling out the big guns and bringing social services into our home. I forced her to sit down, pulling a sobbing Ashley into my lap, murmuring into her ear to keep her eye on Mom and not break contact. In the end Ashley's tears and her wide sad eyes, which could tear even the most grown man in two, had broken Mom down, and she agreed to counseling.

So, every Tuesday, Thursday and Saturday, Mom's counselor came to our home, talking to her for an hour. It usually involved a lot of crying and angry outbursts on Mom's part, and she would always be moody once the counselor left, but surprisingly, she refused to drown her sorrows with drink. And for that I was proud of her, and I told her. Every day.

It was a Thursday, and the doorbell rang, signaling that Aimee, Mom's counselor, was here. I threw on a loose pair of pants and chucked my towel around my neck, jogging down the stairs and pulling the door open.

"Hey, Kane," she greeted me sweetly, and I smirked as her light blue eyes raked over my half-naked form.

As a guy I had to appreciate Aimee's looks. I would be lying if I said she wasn't hot. She was dressed in a tight black pencil skirt which reached just above the knees, and a tight white collared shirt, the top two buttons undone, revealing a black camisole underneath. Her blonde hair was in a ponytail on the left side of her shoulder, and her ridiculously high black heels brought her almost level with me.

Yeah, she was hot alright, and I was pretty sure she knew it too, but I wasn't interested—another factor which just proved I loved Suranne. Prior to Suranne entering my life, the only thought in my mind would've been taking this blonde upstairs. But now, every time she greeted me and gave me that cocky smirk and a raise of her neat, thin eyebrow, I just wanted to go see Suranne. To feel her wavy mahogany hair and wrap my arms around her tiny waist and just kiss the hell out of her, which is what I usually did whenever Aimee came over.

"Hey Aim's," I smirked and stood to the side, gesturing for her to come in. I chuckled under my breath as she slowly brushed past me, and walked towards the living room, making effort to sway her hips in that tiny-ass skirt.

I sighed and shook my head lightly, following after her and kissing Mom on the cheek briefly.

"I'll be back later tonight, Mom. Keep up the good work, I'm proud of you," I murmured to her softly and she smiled back at me. Her eyes, the same color as mine, were clear and hopeful, no longer poisoned by alcohol.

"I hope you bring her home at some point, Kane. Your sister and I would like to meet this infamous lady," she scolded and I couldn't help but grin at her. If only she knew how many times I had brought Suranne home.

"Soon," I assured her, dashing up the stairs to grab a black cotton T-shirt from my room. Pulling it over my still damp hair, I hustled back down the stairs, called out a swift "bye," and headed for my car. I sighed and turned the ignition, always getting a tiny thrill at the purr of my engine. I loved my car.

Pulling out of the drive, I wove through the streets, putting the gear in neutral as I got caught at a stop light. I drummed my fingers on the wheel, waiting for it to turn green and felt my phone vibrating in my pocket. I retrieved it, reading the latest text.

*Where are you?*

I smirked and tapped in my reply.

*I'M ON MY WAY, SOMEONE'S EAGER HUH?*

My phone signalled a new text within seconds.

*Whatever, just hurry up*

I chuckled as my fingers worked over the buttons.

*I KNOW U WANT MORE BABY, DON'T GOTTA LIE*

Like the last, the reply was immediate.

*You wish lol. My aunt just left. Hurry the bloody hell up!*

I smiled, shaking my head. She knew I loved it when she got all feisty and shit. Someone honked their horn from behind, shouting at me to move my car, and I realized the light had changed. I pulled away and sped the rest of the way there. As soon as I pulled up to her aunt's house and got out of my car she was out the door and running at me, jumping into my arms with such force that she knocked me back against the side of my car.

"Hey," I laughed, wrapping my arms tightly around her waist making sure she didn't fall.

"Hey," she breathed against my neck. I smiled as her soft voice washed away everything around us. It was just Suranne and me. "I missed you," she murmured as she lifted her head and locked her eyes with mine.

Those damn eyes.

I smirked and leaned forward, softly pressing my lips against hers.

"You only saw me like three hours ago at school," I whispered against her lips and she hummed, tightening her arms around my neck, pulling my bottom lip between her teeth, which of course made me groan. She knew I dug that shit.

"Didn't you miss me, too?" she pouted up at me, her eyes all wide and sad. I felt her expression tugging at my heart and narrowed my eyes at her. She really knew how to get to me. I exhaled a shaky breath and could see her lips twitching into a smirk—she knowing she had me but was trying her hardest to keep her composure.

"Don't give me that look, Suranne. You know I missed the hell outta you," I muttered, raising an eyebrow as she grinned and pressed her lips softly to mine. I brushed my tongue across her lower lip and she sighed, opening her mouth to me, causing me to hum in approval. Our tongues swirled as she laced her fingers in my hair and massaged lightly. It felt so good that I nearly purred like a damn cat. I groaned into her mouth as my jeans became uncomfortable and I pulled away, gasping for air as I lowered my lips to her ear.

"I want you."

She giggled and sighed as I carried on kissing her neck.

"Wasn't yesterday enough?" she breathed, tilting her head, giving me better access to her neck and gripping my hair tightly. I smirked and pulled away, pecking her on the lips once, softly.

"I'm whipped, what can I say?" I shrugged lightly. It was true—every free moment I had with Suranne, I wanted her. Every time we spoke on the phone, I wanted her. When we had separate classes at school, I wanted her. Hell, I wanted her even when I had her.

She tightened her legs around my waist, smirking as I dropped my head to her shoulder.

"Hmmm," she hummed and kissed down my jaw line before unlocking her tight grasp around me and sliding her legs back down to the ground. I sighed and closed my eyes tightly. She was such a tease.

"Now look what you did." Gesturing to my pants, I tilted my head at her, shaking it mockingly. "What are you gonna do about it, baby?" I stalked toward her slowly as she backed away from me toward her front door.

"Nothing," she smirked back.

"Really?" I raised an eyebrow, taking another step forward as she took another step back. I lowered my voice as I got closer. "That isn't what you said to me last night, Suranne. In fact, I remember you begging," I spoke roughly and flicked my tongue against my lower lip as my eyes raked over her body.

She blushed and averted her gaze to the sidewalk, carrying on with backward steps as I got closer and closer. I chuckled at the redness of her cheeks, amazed at how she could suddenly change into someone timid and shy.

"Kane . . ." she breathed coyly and I closed my eyes, groaning at how her soft voice, thick with her British accent, sent a shiver ripping through my body.

"Yeah?" I choked, eyes still closed as I heard her back coming into contact with the front door. I took two more steps towards her and let her scent swallow me whole.

"We have to go," she breathed heavily against me, and I nuzzled her neck, dragging my nose in a line up to her ear. "Not yet," I whined softly, inhaling her irresistible scent. I placed my hand on her hips and massaged the skin there, the warmth of her body burning through my fingertips and I sighed into her neck. I felt like I just wanted to burrow up inside of her and never leave.

"Kane, as much as I would like to pull you into my now empty home, and have my wicked way, we have a certain someone to pick up," she sighed, her body completely contradicting her words as she pushed herself against me.

"She doesn't finish for another twenty minutes," I mumbled, as my hands continued their journey over her hips, brushing her stomach lightly and sliding up towards the underside of her breasts.

I loved those damn things.

"*Kane*," she warned, and I sighed pulling away and frowning like a little kid, unable to help myself. I wanted her and she was leaving me hanging. I felt like stomping my foot.

She rolled her eyes and leaned up on her toes, brushing her lips against mine but I stood my ground, lips firmly closed, and arms folded over my chest. With a sigh she wrapped her arms around my neck, mewling at my lack of reaction which, of course, broke me down and I ended up winding my arms around her, cradling her tightly and kissing her softly.

She laughed against my lips, the sound automatically warming me and making me smile like some goofy-ass moron.

"OK, we really should go, I'm kinda nervous."

My face became serious and I pulled away, frowning down at her questioningly. "Why would you be nervous? She's just my sister."

She averted her gaze and shrugged, biting her lip nervously. "Yeah, I know but. . . what if she doesn't *like* me?" she murmured. I gazed at her softly, opening my mouth to say those three damn words that I wanted to tell her so badly.

But all that came out was an empty, gusty sigh.

I took her hand gently in mine and gave her a sad smile, my mind still angry that my mouth just wasn't working. I pressed my lips very lightly to her forehead.

"Come on baby, you'll be fine," I said reassuringly, my mind knowing that Ashley would love the crap outta her.

Just as much as I did.

# 26. FROM NERVOUSNESS TO HAPPINESS

## Suranne

"Kane, I'm not so sure about this," I murmured. We were in the parking lot of Kane's sister's school. He was leaning against the side of his car and he had placed his hands on my hips and pulled me flush against him, so that my back was to his chest, his long, toned arms were wrapped around my waist, and his chin rested on my shoulder.

"Quit being a wuss," he mumbled against my shoulder, lifting his head and placing a quick kiss there before resting his chin back against it. The light stubble tickled my skin deliciously and I shuddered as he turned his head and nuzzled my neck.

"But you said how close you two were; won't she be a bit . . . protective?" I wasn't sure why I was so scared of a twelve-year-old girl, but I didn't want her to feel threatened by me; especially after losing her father, I didn't want her to think she would be losing her brother as well.

Kane sighed and squeezed his arms around me as he peppered subtle kisses against my neck and across my shoulder.

"Suranne, you're all she ever talks about. She was the one who kept nagging me to bring you here in the first place. Quit bitchin', baby."

"I'm not bitchin'," I grumbled back at him and went to release his grip, but he laughed and shook his head.

"*Wooah*, no you don't," he laughed, pulling me back against his chest and holding me firmly against him. "You ain't goin' nowhere. And you know you were bitchin'," he mumbled into my neck. I felt him inhale as he dragged his nose up my jugular and pressed a soft kiss just below my ear.

"Are you sniffing me?" I asked, my voice feigning shock.

He hummed and carried on his attack on my neck. Occasionally I felt his tongue dart out. "Can't help it. You smell too good," he muttered and I craned my neck, twisting my head so I could kiss him. I was about to turn around so I could wrap my arms around his neck when I heard someone call out to us.

"Kaanne!"

Kane grunted, pulled away abruptly and cursed under his breath as he released his arms from around my waist and peered around the lot, trying to decipher where the voice, which I assumed belonged to his sister, had come from.

He quickly kissed my cheek and I watched nervously as he jogged off towards a petite girl carrying what looked to be a heavy backpack on her shoulder. She had her brown hair up in a loose ponytail that bounced against her shoulder as she walked towards Kane. I watched as he mussed her hair and she slapped him. I couldn't help but smile as he grabbed her from behind and tickled her torso, causing her to drop her bag as she squealed and tried to slap his hands away.

He stopped his attack on the poor girl, but stayed crouched behind her, his arms wrapping around her small waist as she stood between his legs and he whispered something in her ear. Their eyes darted to me as he continued speaking to her softly. I felt my stomach flutter with nerves as she twisted her head and asked him something.

God, what was he *saying* to her? After he nodded, she turned back to me, her lips curving up into a wide smile as Kane released his grip. She came running up to me and I fidgeted with my hands as she got closer.

"Hey, Suranne," she breathed, energetically. I looked closely at her face and couldn't help but smile at the similarities between her and Kane. She had the same large brown eyes and the same cute crinkles at the side of her eyes when she smiled. Small freckles dotted her nose and I felt my lips smile back.

"Hey, Ashley, your brother tells me a lot about you," I murmured gently, watching as her eyes gleamed when I mentioned Kane. She continued smiling and twisted her head to look over her shoulder at Kane, who was slowly walking towards us with Ashley's backpack in his hand.

She turned back to me and leaned in close to my ear. "Kane talks a lot about you, too," she whispered and I laughed softly. Kane peered at us suspiciously, his eyes narrowing as he stopped in front of us. "What are you two talking about?" he asked firmly, but I saw his eyes light up with amusement as he gazed at us.

With a casual shrug I looked down at Ashley and winked, then I looked up at Kane.

"Nothing. Nothing at all."

I heard Ashley breathe a quiet laugh and Kane cocked an eyebrow up at me disbelievingly, to which I smirked in response.

"Whatever," he replied nonchalantly and opened the back door to let Ashley get in. "Come on dipshit, time to go home," he went to muss her hair again but she stamped on his foot just before jumping in the car and shutting the door so Kane couldn't get her back.

I laughed vindictively and his head snapped towards me.

"You think that's funny, huh?" he asked roughly, his gaze intense.

"Yes," I smirked back. He stalked slowly towards me, his eyes dark. He placed his hand on my hip and ducked his head so that his lips were close to my ear.

"Don't think I won't get you back. We'll see who's laughing later on." He breathed raggedly in my ear before he gently tugged at my lobe with his teeth. My breathing hitched and just as I was about to place my hands on his chest he pulled away and walked around to his side of the car, leaving me standing there breathing heavily, my mind in a daze.

I glanced in the back window and saw Ashley smirking up at me, looking exactly like her brother when he did that. I smiled back at her and cleared my throat, getting in the car.

Kane started up the engine and glanced at me quickly, chuckling. I glared at him meaningfully, but he just gave me that special crooked grin, knowing I couldn't stay angry at him when he did that. My face went soft and he reached for my hand over the console, his chocolate-brown eyes bright and twinkling with an emotion commonly found in other people, but something I had never seen in him before.

I smiled up at him, realising that for the first time in what I was guessing had been three long years, Kane Richards was genuinely happy.

# 27. Drowning In The Bitter Darkness

## Kane

"Mr. Richards, if you could be so kind as to concentrate in my class, perhaps you could tell me what $x$ represents on the scatter graph?" Mr. Horgan raised his bushy brows at me and folded his arms as he waited for an answer.

I narrowed my eyes and looked down at the diagram on my desk.

"0.23," I muttered with a smirk, pretty confident that I had the answer. Bushy Brows nodded curtly, wrote the answer on the board, and then continued to lecture us on some other kind of crap related to math.

Glancing at the clock, I sighed, realizing there were only 10 minutes left till I could leave this damn class, and see her.

Suranne.

These past few weeks had been, undeniably, bliss for me. Mom was still getting counseling, and looking better every day. Ashley absolutely loved Suranne, and they spent every waking moment together. Well, that is when she wasn't at school, or in my bedroom. Or in her bedroom. Or on my desk. Or even on my piano.

Yeah, my girl loved that piano.

I couldn't explain how I was feeling and how most things seemed to be working out for us. Even school had calmed down a notch. People didn't stare as much, in fact they got used to it. They had no choice, because my lips were connected to Suranne's whenever I got the chance, and I didn't care who was watching us.

What was weirder was that I didn't even hold any animosity toward Kate anymore. Ever since our confrontation, and my meltdown after Suranne left with her instead of me, it was like something inside of me had just let loose. Like I had released all the crap I had been holding inside for so damn long towards her, and now all I felt was. . . calm.

And it was thanks to my girl for that.

So yeah, these six weeks or so had, in one way, been heaven.

However.

And yeah, there was a *however*, because if you looked under all the smiles, and kisses, and calm feelings, and great sex, things looked bleak and damn right ugly.

Although my mom had been getting help and was doing better every day, the chick who was counseling her was getting worse.

In the space of these six weeks, Aimee had given me countless hints that she wants me. And yeah, I'm not surprised. I may love my girl, but I'm still big headed and I know that chicks think I'm hot. But the hints I would give her that I was with someone just *wouldn't* deter her. She still made subtle passes, sometimes even being bold enough to "accidentally" brush her hand against the crotch of my jeans as she passed. Her clothes were getting more and more tight and skimpy, but no matter what I said, she just didn't let up.

And this was stressing me out, because although I would never do anything with her, I also hadn't told Suranne about these attempts. I should have, but I knew it would result in some screwed girly cat fight or something. And I didn't need that shit.

But that wasn't all.

Even though I was glad my little sister loved Suranne, Ashley was becoming more and more of a cockblocker for me these days. It was pretty much impossible for me and Suranne to be together in my room if Ashley knew she was there. She would literally bang on the door till Suranne agreed to come out and hang with her. So, recently I've had to resort to sneaking her in just so we can have some quality time. Her aunt still doesn't trust us so we can only go back to her place if she's at work or out somewhere.

So yeah, at the moment, the action I was getting was minimal, and coupled with the crap about Aimee, I was getting more and more worked up.

But guess what? That still wasn't all.

Although school had become a bit calmer, and I held no animosity towards Kate, that sure as hell didn't mean that she didn't hold any towards me. But I could deal with that. I didn't give a damn if she hated me.

What I *couldn't* deal with was the hate she and Lawrence were steering toward Suranne.

Well, I wouldn't say Lawrence hated her, more like gave her the puppy dog act, hoping that she might throw her arms around his neck and *damn* . . .

Just the thought pissed me off.

And so all this was stressing my girl out, and as much as she plastered a brave smile on her face, I could see the tension in her body and the tiredness in her eyes. I tried comforting her whenever I could, but for some reason, sometimes, this pissed her off even more.

But guess what? Yeah, you guessed it. That still wasn't it.

Because nothing, not the stress she was getting from Kate and Lawrence, or the stress I was getting from Aimee and my cockblocking sister could overtake the bigger problem that was looming ahead.

One day ahead, to be precise.

Tomorrow would be the fourth anniversary of my father's death.

And if that day turned out like it had for the past three years, then tomorrow was going to be bad.

Extremely bad.

I knew that all of mom's counseling would pretty much go down the drain, and she would lose herself in a pure, clear bottle of Grey Goose Vodka, and for one day, just for one day I wouldn't blame her.

In fact, every previous year, I had joined her.

So yeah, I was starting to lose it. I could already feel the deep depression mounting, the ebbing ache threatening to rip out of my chest, rearing its ugly black head to overtake my humanity. I could feel the cold substance slowly trickling through my veins. I could feel myself slowly disappearing, and becoming a dark, snappy asshole who wouldn't be held responsible for his actions.

And like I said before, it scared the shit out of me.

Because, unlike the past three years, I now had someone I truly cared about. Someone I truly loved.

And tomorrow I knew, just *knew* I would throw it all way. But there was nothing I could do to stop it. It was like once the clock hit 12:01 a.m. on April 12th, I became someone completely different. I had let it happen for three years straight. The force was too strong.

The bell ringing through the school declaring freedom for students to go to lunch snapped me out of my thoughts. I grabbed my stuff, pushing past everyone to get to the cafeteria first. I walked briskly, focused on getting to Suranne as quickly as possible, hoping that her presence would grate away this coldness I could feel building inside of me. She had healed me before; I could only pray that she was strong enough to pull us through the next seventy-two hours.

I chucked my books on a table once I hit the cafeteria, glaring at anyone who might dare to take my seat and went into the lunch line to get food for Suranne and myself. As I started filling a tray with what I knew she liked, I could feel a weird tingle swirl through my spine, and smiled warmly to myself as I deciphered its meaning.

She was here.

I paid for the food and turned around, smirking, as my eyes rested on the sexy-ass girl sitting down at our table, her creamy pale legs crossed and her elbow on the table, her palm holding up her chin as she smiled sweetly at me.

I felt the familiar pleasant, dull ache throbbing in my chest every time I looked at her, and just like always, I felt the words jumble around in my head, wrapping around my tongue, desperate to be released.

Yeah. I still couldn't tell her I loved her. And today, of all days, I really wished I could, before tomorrow came and I screwed it all up.

"Hey," she breathed as I placed the food on the table and sat down next to her. She frowned at the tray and narrowed her eyes.

"Kane, I told you to stop buying lunch for me. I was about to go up there once you came back."

I couldn't help but smile, she sounded so sexy when she was angry.

"Too late," I shrugged and held the apple out to her, giving her a pleading grin.

She rolled her eyes but took it anyway, her lips twitching up into a smile. "Thank you," she murmured softly, sending a shiver through me. Even after two months her voice still turned me on.

I leaned forward and brushed my lips against hers, deeply breathing in her sweet scent. "You're welcome," I whispered against her mouth, and gave her one last chaste kiss before I pulled away and picked up my pizza.

"So, tomorrow's Saturday. What do you wanna do?" she asked nonchalantly.

"Nothing," I blurted out sharply, my voice cold and acidic. The dark, black force was scratching inside my skin, stretching my nerves as soon as she mentioned tomorrow. I took a deep breath, trying to will away my irrational anger and hold on to whatever calm piece of myself I had left.

Looking at Suranne, I could immediately feel the guilt wash through me, sweeping through my body and pushing back the darkness to its hidden confines. I sighed deeply and shook my head, lifting my arms towards her.

"Come here," I murmured, but she looked hesitant. I could see the hurt in her eyes and I groaned at my own stupid actions. It had started already.

"Please baby, come here." I spoke quietly, and this time she relented, sliding off of her chair and into my lap. She wrapped her arms around my neck and I pulled her to me tightly, sighing as her familiar sweet smell washed over me and calmed my insides.

"I'm sorry," I whispered into her ear as she rested her little head against my neck, her soft hair tickling against my skin.

"Tomorrow, just . . . won't be a good day for me," I muttered bitterly and shook my head, trying to stay focused and not lose myself to the painful anger that was desperate to surge freely through my veins.

"Why?" she asked softly, and I had to choke on my words, trying not to tell her to mind her own business. I was close to losing it, and it was only lunchtime. I took another deep breath, and nuzzled her silky hair, hoping that the smell and texture would keep me grounded, and in control of my emotions.

"Tomorrow will be . . ." I swallowed heavily, trying to push down the lump in my throat so I could choke out the damn words. "Four years," I breathed raggedly, hoping she understood because I wouldn't be able to elaborate any more than that.

"Oh," she breathed, her voice sad but understanding. She hugged me tighter for a second and I squeezed her gently in return, silently thanking her for not pressing the matter. And that was how we spent lunch, Suranne in my lap as I held onto her in silence, neither of us moving, speaking, or even eating. Just being together.

I appreciated it, because I couldn't help but feel like if she spoke or moved I would crack. And I really didn't want to.

But obviously, school had other plans, and the bell sounded loudly, signaling the end of lunch. I gritted my teeth and balled my hands into fists, holding back my anger because it would be crazy to want to snap at a stupid bell.

Suranne gave me one last squeeze and sighed, lifting herself up and grabbing her bag. She gave me a sad smile and leaned down, pressing her lips to mine while I sat still, stopping myself from just grabbing her face and kissing the hell out of her, not wanting to let her leave. Wanting to beg her to steer me through today and tomorrow so that I didn't go off the deep end.

After the second bell rang she pulled away, ran her hand gently through my hair with another sad smile before walking to her next class. As soon as she was gone, I felt worse. Emptier, colder, and darker. I understood that although her presence didn't eliminate the dark inside of me completely, she definitely toned it down.

I quickly got up and grabbed my books before running after her. I spotted her small frame walking down the halls and called out, causing her to stop and turn around. Her eyes widened in surprise and then her face relaxed into a curious smile.

Catching up to her, I pulled her into my arms and held her to me for a few seconds, sighing as I felt the calmness returning.

She was definitely what I needed.

I pulled away and cradled her face in my hands.

"Come see me tomorrow? I know what I said before, but I don't think I can do it alone . . ." I whispered, ducking my head so I was eye level with her.

She bit her lip thoughtfully and gave me a hesitant nod, her brows furrowing with worry but I ignored that, grinning at her in relief before pushing my lips to hers, and kissing her roughly. I slid my tongue along hers passionately, not caring that we were in the hallway of our school and that there were probably some nosy pricks staring.

I pulled away, desperate for air, both of us breathing heavily. I smiled warmly down at her, wanting to hide in the depths of her calming gray eyes. She smiled back as I released my arms from around her. I tilted my head in the direction of her classroom, and as soon as she disappeared into her class, I felt the darkness seeping back, even stronger, causing me to gasp from its intensity.

What the hell was *wrong* with me? I had never gotten this bad so soon.

I stumbled down the hallway, my hand pushing against my chest and the fierce, painful feeling there as I made my way to the parking lot. I wouldn't make it through class, that was for sure.

It felt like tunnel vision or something. My mind couldn't comprehend what was going on and before I knew it, I found myself in my car about to turn the ignition. I frowned, not even remembering entering the lot, but the pain in my chest, the swirling, forceful anger that seeped through my veins had risen tenfold and I couldn't concentrate. I was losing my mind and the only thing I could think of was getting home and finding a bottle of Grey Goose.

My breathing was labored, and my eyes were shifting in different directions as I drove home. It felt like I was going numb, my hands steering and changing gears robotically while my foot pressed down on the gas without my giving it a thought. I could feel myself slipping dramatically, and I let out a choked sob in an attempt to get myself together again. It wasn't even tomorrow yet and I was losing myself. Once again, it was like I folded and found myself in my kitchen, without any memory of getting there. There was a half full glass in my hand, and the bottle of GG on the side. My hand lifted of its own volition, and the last thing I remembered was the cool crystal glass touching my lips before the raging force inside my chest took over.

I faintly remember whispering Suranne's name as I drowned in the dark, bitter abyss that consumed me at this same time, every year.

# 28. A DARK CASE OF PATHETIC FALLACY

## Suranne

"**Y**ou still want me to come over? x'

I shut my phone, tossed it on the bed, and sat on the edge. I had tried ringing Kane after school yesterday when I realised he had gone home early, but he didn't pick up so I decided to leave him alone. I didn't want to come across as one of those clingy types, but Kane rang me almost every night. That is, if he wasn't with me at the time.

I couldn't even describe how happy I had been feeling recently. The Kane Richards of late was such a contrast to the person I was warned about and had observed my first few weeks here. He was so happy and loving that I couldn't help but smile just thinking about him.

Every kiss and every touch from him left me breathless. The array of emotions that would surge through me every time we were together was indescribable. And it was pretty obvious since my first day here, from the string of girls that were always chasing after him, that he had to be good.

But I never thought he would be *that* good. I felt like an addict and he was the most delicious, euphoric, toxic drug. I could never have enough. And the look in his eyes, all dark, full of desire and lust, always drove me crazy.

However, our alone time had recently become very limited. Admittedly I was having withdrawal symptoms, sometimes even snapping at him, and getting irritated when he tried to reassure me that we would be alone soon. It wasn't his fault, but I couldn't exactly blame his sister. She was amazing, and I was so relieved that she and their mother both liked me.

Looking back, my first thoughts on Kane's mum had been bitter, disgusted at how she could be so selfish. Drowning her sorrows in alcohol and leaving her son to pick up the pieces. When she first greeted me, my reply came out harsher than expected, but the shame and sorrow that flickered in her eyes— large, brown expressive eyes like Kane's—just made me feel guilty. She looked so healthy and happy now that she was getting counselling, and we got along perfectly.

But there was an uneasy twist in my stomach as I thought about what this day meant to Kane. Today marked four years since his father's death, and the pain and grief in his eyes yesterday seemed to be reflected through pretty much everything I laid my eyes on. The sky was grey and a strong wind whipped the tree branches in various directions outside of my window, casting an almost eerie shadow in my room. I couldn't fathom why a feeling of panic and nervousness was spreading through me, so I brushed it off, scowling at my childish fears before padding off to the bathroom to get ready to see him.

As soon as I got out of the shower and dried my hair, I reached for my phone, still lying on the bed. No new messages. He still hadn't texted back. I wondered if it was best for me to stay here and wait for him to contact me instead, but he had told me he wanted me with him today. He needed me to get him through this, and I wanted to be there to support him, too.

Dark clouds rolled in outside of my window, causing me to hit the light so I could see to get dressed. It was only like two in the afternoon, and from the look of things outside the window it was likely to rain today.

I sighed, deciding to just go to Kane's and talk to him, or just sit there in silence. Anything he needed me to do, I would do.

Once dressed I went downstairs into the kitchen and saw my aunt sitting at the table reading a newspaper. She lifted her head and smiled brightly as I went to sit opposite her.

"Hey Kiddo, what ya doin' today?" she asked, licking her thumb lightly before turning the page.

"Kane," I mumbled, and she frowned at me disapprovingly. For some reason she wasn't all that keen on him and didn't always approve of me going over to visit him, but I told her that his mum and sister would be there and she stopped grumbling.

"Still," she muttered dryly, and I groaned in irritation.

"It's the anniversary of his father's death today, give him a break."

She nodded but the frown was still on her face as she turned her attention back to the paper. I rang for a cab, because I still wasn't familiar with the bus system here, and it was way too far for me to walk. When it came, I kissed my aunt on the cheek, whispering a goodbye before running out, sliding into the backseat, giving the man Kane's address.

I watched the sky as we drove, wondering if it was going to storm, and something told me to turn around. To go back home and wait until tomorrow, but once again, I shook my head.

This was Kane we were talking about. I had no reason to feel like this.

We pulled up to his driveway, and I paid the man, thanking him as I got out. The dark sky set a gloomy hue of uncertainty upon the house, its bricks looking almost sinister. I took a deep breath and pushed myself to walk up to the front door.

I rang the doorbell, pushing away the sickness that rolled around in my stomach and the urge to suddenly heave from the nerves that were spiralling within me. I waited for ages, just standing there, my breathing heavy until I heard footsteps and a low, mumbled "I'm coming," which I knew belonged to Kane. I smiled brightly as I heard him unlock the door before he pulled it open.

My smile disappeared as soon as I laid eyes on him. He was dressed in dark jeans, which hung deliciously low on his hips, and his torso and feet were bare. His hair was a mess, just the way I liked it, but his appearance didn't make me squirm with want. I didn't feel a rush of desire stab through me at his half-naked appearance. I frowned looking at him; there was something unusual and distinct about his . . . stance?

He let me in, and I narrowed my eyes at the tall glass in his hand, half filled with a clear liquid. I knew Kane only drank bottled water.

"Jesus, Kane, is that all *vodka?*" I asked irritably, knowing how he usually despised any form of alcohol and the effects it had. You only had to look at his mother for proof of that, and the fact that he was drinking right now wasn't a good sign. By the way he was swaying slightly, I guessed it wasn't his first glass.

He dropped his head to look at the glass and shrugged lazily before shuffling up the stairs without a word. I stared after him nervously, then turned around and closed the door. Taking a deep breath, I shut my eyes and rested my head on the door for a few seconds, and with a groan I pulled myself away and followed

Kane up the stairs to his bedroom door, which was slightly ajar. I pushed it open and anxiously stepped in, but scanning his room, I found it empty. I walked further in, stopping at the middle. A loud bang over my shoulder caused me to jump. I swivelled around to find the bedroom door slammed shut and Kane leaning against it. His face cold and calm as he gazed at me blankly.

"Sorry to scare you, baby," he spoke, his voice calm, and chillingly *different*.

"Uh . . . I—it's OK," I stammered weakly, frowning at him as I tried to place what it was about his appearance and demeanour that had changed.

He laughed bitterly as he raised the glass to his lips and downed it in one gulp. I gaped at him, shocked.

"Umm . . . Kane," I spoke softly, but his head snapped up in my direction, and his eyes narrowed at me menacingly.

"What?" he hissed, his voice dark, his lips curled up into a sneer as his fingers wrapped around the glass even more tightly, his knuckles protruding against the skin.

I swallowed heavily, unwilling to let my inner fear overtake me. This was a bad day for him. I needed to remember that.

"Maybe you should . . . put the glass down." I spoke softly, slowly, my eyes gentle as they roamed over his face. Something about his features was different but I couldn't quite place what.

"Fuck what I should do," he muttered into the now empty glass, a displeased frown upon his unfamiliar face. I took a cautious step closer toward him and his eyes immediately flickered back to mine.

And then I gasped.

It was his eyes. That's what was so different about him, the thing I hadn't been able to put my finger on. They were no longer the light, smooth, swirling chocolate-brown that showed a million emotions.

They were black, but not in lust, or desire.

They were cold. Hard. Distant.

He continued to glare at me, as if I was some enemy about to attack him and he was warning me off. His eyes screamed at me, burned at me, but all the while, they remained empty and unfeeling. They communicated nothing and everything at the same time. This was not Kane. This was someone dark and dangerous; my inner instincts were shrieking at me to be on alert.

"What you doin' just standin' there baby? Hmm? I don't even get a kiss *hello* anymore?"

His bone-chillingly cold voice sent a shiver down my spine, his words sounded automatic, unnatural. They had a slight mocking edge, as if they were part of some hidden joke. He tilted his head, giving me his signature crooked grin which, if it had really been Kane, would have made me blush, smile shyly, and just want to kiss his face off, but now?

That grin just looked . . . *Evil.*

I took a deep breath, and stepped closer, watching him closely the whole time. His eyes still had that blank look that screamed at me to back off, but the smirk on his face increased with every step closer I took. My body felt torn, desperately wanting to comfort him and snap him out of this place he was in, and at the same time desperately wanting to run the other way.

I was having an inner battle. Should I let myself be comforted in the feel of his arms around me, or stay put and gently coax him out of his state of detachment?

But my internal questions were futile, because without even realising it, I had moved halfway across the room, as if drawn to him like a magnet without my permission, and even though the look on his face was alarming, I found myself continuing to put one foot in front of the other.

Kane's black and vacant eyes continued to smoulder at me as I walked over to him, hypnotised by his stare. He must have realised this also, because I could have sworn a ghostly, amused chuckle escape his curled lips, and filled the air with a thick layer of tension.

## 29. THE FINAL SNAP OF A WITHERED ROPE

### Suranne

J ust a kiss.

It's just a kiss.

I'd kissed Kane plenty of times before, so why now did I feel so apprehensive, reluctant?

But if I felt so reluctant, why was I right in front of Kane, letting him wrap his arms stiffly around my waist?

The thudding in my chest was uncontrollable as Kane's lips moved around mine. He lifted an arm, and threaded his fingers through the back of my hair, pushing my face closer to his whilst he kissed me with abandon. And although I knew this was wrong, the tingling sensation whenever he kissed me was still in full force. But I knew we needed to talk about this. I had to see at least a flicker of compassion or love in Kane's currently dead, blank eyes.

"No, Kane, I—I—I . . ." I was too breathless to finish my sentence, by this time, his lips were trailing down my neck, and across my throat. The feeling against my skin was amazing, as usual. I shuddered from the tingling of his kisses and tried my best to hold back a moan, but it was too much to bear. I bit my lip but a very quiet moan still escaped. I felt his lips curve up into a smile against my skin, and he breathed a sinister laugh.

"It's OK, Suranne," he murmured against my skin, his voice monotone, lifeless. "Just let your body go with it. Every girl I have caves in the end."

Mmm. Wait, *what?* I pushed away from his grip and narrowed my eyes at him.

"What did you just say?" I hissed, glaring fiercely at him as a stab of anger and hurt pierced me.

"Well come on, babe, we both know I'm irresistible, you might as well stop fighting it," he chuckled darkly, his face holding no emotion whatsoever.

I stared at him in shock, my jaw agape. *Never* had he talked about me as if I was one of his general 'girls'. *Ever.*

"You drunken *pig!*" I retorted, clenching my teeth in anger and to get a grip on my emotions.

"Mmm, you know you sound so hot when you're angry. Call me that again."

He smirked, leaning his head back against the door, his startlingly black eyes glaring down at me. I took a deep breath and walked closer to him, ignoring the silent shrieking in his eyes warning me to stay back.

"Kane, we need to talk, you *know* that. Please, you're not acting yourself right now," I pleaded, trapping his head in my hands firmly, forcing him to look at me, but his eyes were glassy.

He wasn't Kane right now, but it wasn't until then that I realised just how far away the real Kane, *my Kane*, actually was. I let go of his face and went to move past him, wanting to go downstairs and get a glass of water. A nervous sweat was building up at the nape of my neck and my heart was hammering wildly. I finally understood why I had felt so uneasy on my way here. It was a silent warning that Kane would be like this. I frowned, wondering about his mother's and sister's whereabouts.

As I curled my hand around the brass door handle and pulled it open slightly, Kane's arm shot out, slamming the door closed loudly and I yelped in surprise.

"Where you goin', baby?" He sneered, his brown eyes still black and burning with a foreign, sinister shine as he gazed unseeingly at me. He ran the back of his hand down my cheek and I shivered from his touch, almost recoiling from the dark persona he had become.

"I . . . I think I would like some water," I whispered inaudibly, swallowing heavily and far too afraid to meet his gaze. My chest ached for him, the *real* him, and I could feel a lump in my throat burning beneath my skin.

He hummed, and pushed himself up against me, ducking his head so that his lips were close to my ear.

"I think I would like my father back. But that's not gonna happen, is it?" He spoke sharply, his voice like shining, deadly shards of glass that cut through my heart and left me bleeding for him. My chest was heaving, and I was biting my lip trying to keep the frightened tears at bay, but still he continued.

"I think I'd like to be able to go to bed, and for once . . . just *once*, not have the memories of his death replay through my mind again and again." His voice rose as he spoke, and his tone grew even harsher with every heart-wrenching syllable.

He pulled away and took a few steps back, the anger and unrecognisable pain that blazed in his onyx eyes took my breath away. My stomach tightened in turmoil and I could feel my body shaking under his intense stare.

"I *fucking think*," he spat at me, one of his fists clenched uncomfortably whilst his other was still tightly wrapped around the empty glass, "that I should be able to feel like I done my father proud, but then!" he growled, his eyes no longer focused, staring through me, "I realise I can't. Because every time I come *home*, I have to see how my mother became a careless, depressed, comatose *drunk*!"

I let a sob escape my chest and flinched as he raised his hand that was wrapped around the glass and with undeniable force, slammed it into the wall. The piercing sound of the glass shattering, breaking into tiny pieces, undid me and I fell to the floor, crying and shaking as the fissured pieces of crystal stared back at me from the floor, representing my resolve at that point.

A large thud registered in my ears and I weakly lifted my head, making out Kane's slumped body next to his bed through my hazy tears. He had his knees up, his arms resting on them as his hands held his head. "I . . . fucking . . . think," he murmured weakly, his voice breaking and sending the final spear through my chest, as if I could feel his pain. His shaking form proved to me that he was crying, each sob echoing through the room like a wounded animal begging for assistance. His cries got louder, alternating between sounds of sorrow and pain, to growls of anger and frustration as he combed his fingers through his hair furiously.

On shaky knees, I slowly crawled over to him, my remorseful sniffles mingling with his aggrieved sobs. I took a deep breath once I was a few inches away from him, and lifted my hand to place on his knees.

"Don't." His command was low, cold, and lifeless.

"Kane, I . . ." I trailed off, lost for words and feeling utterly helpless. I didn't know what to do or say that could possibly bring him back. He was too far gone.

"Don't even touch me," he whispered into his hands, his voice one hundred percent monotone and emotionless, which only worried me even more. At least before, I'd been able to hear the irritation in his tone, feel the anger behind his words. But now there was . . . *nothing*. Nothing but lifeless verbs and nouns laced with limp connectors.

It had begun to rain outside; the view from the windows folded into a dark, grey, slithering wet blur as the continuous beating of the rain thudded against the glass, showering the room in a noise of misty hums.

The room became a dull shadow, and I could faintly make out the curve of Kane's jaw and the outline of his unruly dark hair peeking out through his long, toned fingers. I racked my brain for something to say, thinking back to all the times I had helped him before. How I didn't have to think about what to say then, but just came out with whatever was on my mind. I thought about these past few weeks. The sweet, flirty kisses to the full on, passion-filled ones. The light, innocent brushes of his hands, to the meaningful gropes of his slender fingers, each touch sending a surge of desire rushing through my veins.

I thought of his smile, and how just the mere sight of it ignited a warmth in my chest. I thought of the chocolate brown of his eyes, and the endless number of expressions I could distinguish from his stare.

And as these memories filled my mind, they took over my soul. I felt them spread through my limbs, slowly trickling through my veins and filling me up with such an intense emotion that I gasped loudly and formed the only words that were willing to be said. And so I smiled, a large, victorious smile, because I knew these words would do the job. I *knew* that I could fix him again.

"Kane," I breathed, "I love you."

The words slipped from my lips and swirled into the thick air, wrapping around his body and trying to sink into every pore of his skin and consume him like they did me.

I was still smiling as I waited for a change in his position; a sign of his healing, or even a reply so that I could exhale the large breath which I had been holding.

But nothing happened.

The room grew impossibly darker as his silence overtook my words and crushed them, stamping them into the ground as if they never existed. Dread coursed through me, and a silent, lone tear escaped my cheek as a fierce pain spread, making it impossible to even breathe.

"Please Kane . . ." I choked, now reversing the roles and pleading with him to save me instead.

He didn't *move*.

He didn't love me.

And from the still, statue-like form of his position, he showed no sign that he ever would.

The rain was just a light drizzle now as I picked myself up, my body feeling heavy and weak.

He still didn't move when I reached for his bedroom door. Or when I turned the handle.

He remained still when I stepped through the door and turned back to him, standing in his hallway looking in. I slowly shut the door, closing away the image of his marble folded body; my mind flickered to the wrecked glass on the floor, but as I thought about it, the image transformed, until they were no longer pieces of crystal.

But shattered and beaten pieces of a red, fleshy organ no longer situated in the confines of my broken and ruptured chest.

# 30. PAINFUL ULTIMATUM

## Kane

I groaned as a sharp pain shot through my shoulder. "Shit," I muttered, my voice still thick and groggy from sleep as I rubbed my face roughly. I blinked as I tried to come to terms with my whereabouts.

Crap. No wonder I felt so damn stiff. I'd slept on the fucking floor.

I frowned, trying to remember doing that, but came up blank. My mind was hazy and kinda numb. It took a while for me to even remember what day it was . . . or the date.

The date.

I grimaced and racked my brain for the information, but it felt like I had been drugged, and I couldn't remember a damn thing. And I only ever got that shitty feeling once a year, as if my memory of the last twenty-four hours had been completely swiped, leaving only a huge, gaping dark hole which, even with my strained efforts, would only come back to me in stages over the next few hours.

That only happened on April 12th, so it was pretty damn apparent that this was April 13th.

With a groan I lifted myself off the hard floor, wincing as I stretched my cramped muscles, stumbling slightly as I tried to regain my balance. My head was hurting and my mouth tasted like a cocktail of sourness that made me feel sick to my stomach. I continued rubbing my face roughly with my hand, trying to get my bearings when something crunched loudly under the weight of my feet and I felt my skin tear sharply.

"Son of a *bitch*!" I yelled out, gripping my bleeding foot and inspecting it, only to be completely shocked to discover a splintered glass on the floor.

Like a slap in the face, various images assaulted my mind, whirling recklessly in my skull and leaving me breathless.

A pale soft face, cheeks wet, and wide gray eyes shining with tears and unadulterated fear. Wavy mahogany hair falling about gently around her shoulders, which were slumped in what looked to be apprehension.

My fist curled tightly around a clear crystal glass, my tendons screaming out in protest as I smashed the glass against the wall. The shrill shattering of the crystal reverberating through my ears along with a small, fearful whimper from across the room.

A dark panic trickled down my spine as recognition sparked within me at the images of that same face, that same skin, those same eyes, that same thick soft hair.

Suranne.

"No, no, *no*," I murmured to myself, hopping around feverishly, ripping clothes out of closets and dressers, trying to get dressed quickly as my heart beat an uncontrollable staccato in my chest. My head continued to throb along with my bleeding foot but I just gritted my teeth and dealt with it. I couldn't push out the image of Suranne's face from my mind. I remember asking her to come over when we were at school, thinking that she would help. But maybe that hadn't been a good idea. And worst of all, I still couldn't remember everything.

Did I shout at her?

Did I say shit that I didn't mean?

Did I *hurt* her?

My mood was impossibly sour on that day, which is why I always locked myself in my room, but this was more than that. I felt like I had completely lost myself, without a trace of any humanity whatsoever, like I was just coming out of a damn coma.

I absently snatched a Band-Aid from the first aid box in my bathroom, put it on my foot, and continued to get dressed. Slipping on my Nikes, I headed down the stairs. My mom was standing in the kitchen, in a pressed white suit, her hair up in a tight bun.

"Mom?"

She turned and my jaw dropped at how refreshed she looked. I hardly recognized her. She was young, *alive*. Which was something I was not expecting the day after the anniversary of the worst day of our lives.

"Hey honey!" she breathed happily, walking up to me and placing her hand on my cheek briefly before going up the stairs.

"Where the hell were you yesterday?" I called out to her, 'cause if she'd been here, surely she would've stopped me from acting like a crazy prick to Suranne. Surely she would've heard something.

Mom turned around once she reached the top of the stairs and smiled sadly at me.

"Aimee suggested that I have dinner with her last night. I knew that I would need to get out of this house if I was to carry on . . . healing myself. I needed to get away from the . . . memories."

I narrowed my eyes at the mention of Aimee. I was sure that it wasn't routine for therapists to associate with their patients like that. But I couldn't help but be thankful. At least my mom kept herself on track.

God knows why I didn't do the same thing.

"I have to go," I mumbled as the urgency to see Suranne and apologize for whatever I may have done came back to me again.

***

My chest was beating wildly as I pulled up into Suranne's drive. I took a deep breath and threw my car door open, jogging to her front door and banging on it wildly. I knew I wouldn't be in control until I saw her face. I knew these nerves and this ache in my chest wouldn't dissipate until my eyes came into contact with hers, but when the door finally snapped open, it wasn't Suranne standing there. Glaring daggers at me with a ferocious expression was her aunt.

"What the *hell* do you want?" she spat menacingly and I backed up from the venom in her voice.

"Uhh . . . is Suranne here?" I asked in my most polite voice, throwing in a smile just for good measure.

"Not for you she isn't," she replied tersely and folded her arms over her chest.

My eyes widened in shock as I gaped at her.

"Uhh . . . Cou—"

"Ever since yesterday that niece of mine has been a wreck; crying, not eating, and just refusing to leave her room for anything. And I *know* that she was with *you* yesterday, so don't try pulling that innocent crap with me, son. You may be able to get girls to fall for your charming smile, but it sure as hell isn't gonna *work* with me." She was pointing her finger at me viciously now, stepping closer and closer to me with each word.

I held my hands up, palms outward in defense. Her words about Suranne made a knot twist in my stomach and caused the ache in my chest to only get stronger. I was so close to her, I could *feel* it, but I couldn't see her.

I had to see her.

"Mrs. Williams I—"

"*MISS!*" She interrupted me, "I'm not bloody *married!*"

Well damn. *My bad.*

"*Miss* Williams," I corrected, taking on a soft tone, "I honestly didn't realize Suranne was upset, but I really do need to talk to her. It's important."

She opened her mouth to reply when a soft voice carried out from behind her and made my insides swirl with relief.

"It's OK, Aunt Clacy," I heard her whisper softly. I still couldn't see her because her aunt was blocking the goddamn way. "I doubt he'll be staying anyway."

I frowned at that. Why the hell wouldn't I be?

As soon as her aunt moved to the side and revealed Suranne's face, I nearly fell to my knees as several images flashed in my head.

Me, in my bedroom. It was dark and I could hear the rain tapping against the window. I barely registered the raspy sobs in the background. I knew they were close to me but for some reason I couldn't see her. I had my head in my hands. And then I felt my voice ring out in the air. Cold and toneless.

"Don't even touch me."

*Christ.* How could I say that to her?

I winced as I caught my breath and glanced at Suranne's face. She seemed drained; her eyes were red—she had obviously been crying. Her shoulders were slumped and her hands hung limply by her sides. She was wearing a large, baggy white T-shirt and jeans. Her hair was in a messy ponytail on her shoulder, a few strands sticking to the side of her face.

"Jesus," I breathed. I still couldn't deny the uncontrollable pull I had towards her—even if she did look like shit. Her aunt leaned over and whispered in her ear, at which Suranne stiffly nodded, her sunken gray eyes piercing through mine the whole time. Obviously happy with her response, her aunt walked back inside and softly shut the door, but not without giving me an evil glare beforehand.

I took a deep breath and stuffed my hands in my pockets as I gazed at Suranne in remorse.

"Baby . . . I'm *sorry*," I murmured to her, my insides coiled intensely hoping like hell she understood that yesterday just . . . wasn't me.

"I know," she whispered simply, her body still sagging, but her eyes burning brightly at me.

I frowned at her lack of response, but still tried to plead my case.

"Yesterday I . . . just wasn't myself. I mean *Christ*, I can hardly remember anything." I mumbled the last part in frustration, mostly to myself.

She chuckled darkly, "Yeah, well, that's probably due to the ridiculously large amount of *vodka* you consumed," she replied dryly.

I winced and shook my head, taking a step closer towards her. She didn't move a muscle. This was not going well.

"No . . . I mean, yeah . . . that didn't help. But this happens to me every year. I always lose it on April 12th. I always have. I tried to warn you," I muttered.

Her eyes stayed fixed on mine. She remained immobile, her body hardly moving apart from the infinitesimal movement of her chest with each breath.

"I'm so sorry Suranne, honestly I am . . . Christ, I . . ." I trailed off, really wanting to tell her how I felt about her. The feeling was even stronger within me than it had been before. I was certain that it wasn't just some misconception on my part.

I saw something close to hope flicker in her eyes, and her shoulders straightened slightly. "You what?" she asked, her voice louder, stronger.

I gazed at her large gray eyes, which were boring into mine, swirling with anticipation. Her eyebrows were raised, waiting for my response.

"I . . ." I started, trying to force the words out.

They wouldn't come.

I sighed heavily, completely pissed off at my own selfishness and lack of verbal balls, "I'm sorry," I muttered.

Her whole demeanor changed at my words. Her shoulders slumped again, her eyes losing their hopeful sparkle, becoming blank but still burning into mine.

"It wasn't me," I offered again, hoping that was enough to pull her out of her drained state.

"I know," she whispered, "But this is you . . ."

"Yes," I replied firmly, closing the distance between us and placing my fingers underneath her chin, pushing it upwards so she was looking up at me. She closed her eyes and drew in a deep breath, before releasing it steadily. When she opened her eyes again they were vulnerable but determined.

"I love you, Kane."

My mouth fell open at her words, instantly poised to reply. My chest was swimming with warmness; I was elated.

So why couldn't I just *say it back*?

The seconds ticked by, her eyes became more and more vulnerable, and less determined with every breath, then they clouded with tears.

"Suranne, I…" I stuttered, my mind screaming at me to just *say it*. My mouth still gaped at her.

She released my grip and took a few steps back, shaking her head sadly. I followed her.

I would *always* follow her.

"I feel the same Suranne . . . honestly, I *do*!" My eyes pleaded with her to believe me, to understand that I was having some screwed up internal battle between my head and my heart, and that, right now, my head was winning.

"*Tell me*," she cried, her eyes wide and begging. They were reaching out to me, and all I wanted to do was reach back. To tell her I loved her and embrace her. To kiss her and take her up to bed and make her cry out in a good way.

"I *can't*," I whimpered pathetically. As much as I wanted to do all that, my brain just wouldn't *let me*.

I saw Suranne's eyes flash with rejection, before cooling into a steely hard resolve. She nodded at me, regaining control of her emotions and letting out a slow breath.

"Come find me when you can," she whispered before turning around and walking back into her house without another word.

I stared at her door numbly for a few minutes, trying to gather what I felt.

Was I angry? She didn't walk out on me like Kate did. It was more the other way around. She had told me she loved me, begged for me to reciprocate and I just . . . couldn't.

I turned and slowly made my way back to my car, crawling out of her drive and back towards my own home. The silence in the car wrapped around me and brought me down to a depressed level of melancholy as I replayed her words over and over in my mind.

And yet, my own words also replayed themselves in my head, alongside hers.

*I love you, too.*

# 31. From The Outside Looking In

## Suzanne

This was barely survival. The past weeks had just clung to me, every second, every minute, every hour . . . every day wrapping around me tightly, reminding me how he still hadn't come back to me. And yet, each day had drifted by, so sickeningly slow, mocking me and the emptiness I felt inside.

It felt like my whole purpose here had just been sucked into a dark abyss of . . . *nothing*. After week one, my eyes were scratchy and sore from the constant tears. My chest screamed out in painful protest from my racking sobs, and yet, after all of that, at every car door I heard outside my window, or shuffling feet, or voice, or the sound of someone knocking at my door, hope would make an appearance, swirling through my chest and lingering in my heart at the chance it might be him.

It never was.

After week two, there were no more tears to shed, no more sobs to heave, no more anger and pain to let bleed through me and seep into the cracks of my room. I had released everything and become a dry, empty carcass that held no emotion, no laughter, no happiness.

No life.

I drifted through my daily routines blankly. I woke up. I showered. I brushed my teeth. I thanked my aunt for the toast she would make me every morning. I grabbed my book bag and went to school. I weaved through the halls of the building as various other students weaved past me. I blurred through my lessons, I ate lunch—at a different table than the one I used to—and then I came home, did my homework and went to bed, only for the cycle to begin once again.

At the beginning of the third week I heard my aunt on the phone, her tone quiet and worried as she spoke about me. To who I wasn't sure, nor did I really care. I would just stiffly sit on my bed, knees drawn up to my chest, resting my chin on them as I stared at the light purple wall in front of me. Thankfully Kane and I hadn't taken any pictures. I knew that one glance at his perfectly sculptured jaw and flawless features and I would just drown and wouldn't resurface.

And I knew his timetable by heart so it was pretty easy to avoid spotting him in the halls between lessons. Apart from Friday.

Every Friday I had no choice.

Because every Friday, we had the same last lesson.

Which was today.

The last two Fridays I'd ducked my head, closing my eyes and praying he didn't make himself obvious. I could never control the way my heart came to life and beat out of rhythm in my chest whenever he entered the classroom. Regardless of whether my eyes were wide open or smashed shut, I always knew when he was there. My body would just react. I would feel the hair on the back of my neck tingle, my skin would go cold and would get goosebumps, and of course, the telltale sign was my heart.

There was no controlling it when Kane Richards was around.

Of course it didn't help that the whole class would instantly become silent upon his entrance. Most of the school had become aware that there was no more Kane and Suranne, and so the tension was palpable, as if all of the other twenty-five students in the class were holding their breath, peering at Kane, only to turn around and glance at me, then return back to him. I never knew how he looked, or what his facial reaction was. I never lifted my head nor opened my eyes, but a shudder would pass through me when I felt him walk past to his own desk, his ultra sweet cologne drifting up my nose and becoming a sickening poison that obliterated my insides with every breath.

However, there was one good thing that came out of this.

Lawrence.

Over the past couple of weeks he had been my saviour. At first he'd given me disappointed glances and mutters of "I told you so" under his breath, but that quickly changed into glances of remorse and concern, and outright asking if I was OK. He would escort me to all my lessons as I cowered to the edge of the halls and shuffled blankly to my destinations. He was a distraction from the ache, the numbing, dull pain that consumed me since the day Kane stood outside my house.

A clearing of a throat brought me back to the present, and my eyes focused on the concerned, icy blue eyes of Lawrence as he sat in front of me at the lunch table.

"Ya hear me?" he asked softly before crunching on his crisps which, he had informed me earlier, were addressed as 'chips' over here.

I shook my head in apology, "Sorry, what?"

"I said, you gonna be OK last lesson?"

Wincing at his mention of the inevitable lesson with Kane, I quickly nodded, immediately attempting to divert the direction

Lawrence wanted to take the conversation. Luckily, I noticed his eyes flash with understanding and he gave me a slight nod before running his hand through his short hair. The motion sparked memories of Kane doing the exact same thing with his sexy crooked grin after I had sneaked him back to my house one day. He was shirtless, with nothing but my sheet wrapped around his waist, hanging low on his hips. I remembered biting my lip as I took in the ridges of his abs, and couldn't escape the giggle when Kane had caught me ogling and cleared his throat, before leaning forward and kissing me softly on the lips.

I gasped from the pain in my chest and shook the memory from my head. Everything reminded me of him these days.

I just couldn't escape him.

The bell signalled it was time for last lesson, and I begrudgingly lifted myself from the table, gathering my things and smiling warmly at Lawrence when he gingerly put his arm around my shoulder as he guided me down the hall.

"I'm sorry, Suranne," he murmured, his voice regretful as we walked towards the classroom.

I frowned. "What for?"

He sighed and shook his head lightly as we stopped outside the classroom door.

"I'm sorry I wasn't good enough f—"

"No, Lawrence," I interrupted him. I knew what he was going to say, and hearing him bring himself down like that would just fill me with a fat load of guilt. "Don't ever think you're not good enough for someone. If anything, you're too good for people like me."

He smiled at me in thanks, his piercing blue eyes twinkling at me as he leant down quickly, giving me a chaste kiss on the cheek.

"I'll give you a lift home—wait for me in the lot, 'kay?" he replied firmly, raising his brows, waiting for my response. My early arguments that I could easily walk home never satisfied him, so I nodded and he grinned, walking off with a small wave of his hand.

I took a calming breath and steeled myself for another excruciating lesson just a few feet from Kane Richards and unable to do anything about it. As I walked in, the classroom held only a couple of other students and they were the silent, unsocial types, with their noses firmly stuck in their books. I breathed a sigh of relief and went to the back to sit at my desk.

As soon as I sat down, another memory flashed in my head from a few weeks ago. Kane sat on the edge of my desk and I stood between his legs with my back to his chest. He had his arms wrapped around me and his chin resting on my shoulder as he spoke to Alex, one of his basketball friends. I couldn't understand half of the stuff he was saying, so I had just closed my eyes and leaned back into him, smiling as he occasionally pressed his lips softly to my neck, and every time he laughed at something Alex said, he would hold me more tightly against him.

With an angry growl, I fought to hold my tears back as the longing that was screaming underneath my skin urged me to go to him. To feel his arms hold me again, to feel his lips against my skin.

I hadn't realised how long it had actually taken to get a grip on myself, but when I looked up again, the class was full and the teacher was already half way through his lecture. Without realising what I was doing, my head snapped to the side to where Kane's desk was, only to find it empty.

Kane wasn't there.

He rarely missed a lesson, and, although there was a tiny part of me that was silently grateful he wasn't in this particular lesson, the larger part of me felt disappointed. I couldn't help but wonder where he was, what he was doing, why he wasn't here.

Was he sick?

Did he get into a fight?

Was something wrong with his mother, or even worse, his sister?

I stared at the clock for the rest of the lesson, patiently counting down the minutes, and then, finally, the seconds, until the bell rang. I hastily put my books away and grabbed my bag, threw it over my shoulder, and rushed out to the parking lot. I spotted Lawrence leaning against his car, his eyes fixed on the entrance, before he noticed me and smiled widely. I smiled back and made my way over to him, not able to help how every few seconds my eyes would dart to different parts of the parking lot, looking for Kane's car, or Kane himself.

"Hey, how'd it go?" Lawrence asked me, taking my bag from my shoulder and throwing it in the back seat of his car. I shrugged, once again looking over my shoulder to see if I could notice him.

"He wasn't there," I mumbled distractedly.

"Really? Huh, he was in practice this morning, and I could have sworn I saw him at lunch," Lawrence replied and I snapped my head at him, watching as he rubbed his jaw thoughtfully. I saw his eyes slowly drift past me before his whole body stiffened and his eyes widened. I saw a brief flash of panic before his face relaxed into a calm mask and he focused back on me.

"Come on, let's go . . . get in," he instructed, opening the passenger door, his eyes flickering behind me every other second.

"What is it?" I asked softly, frowning at his sudden change in behaviour. I went to turn around but his hand clamped down on my shoulder.

"Come on, Suranne, let's just go, yeah?" he said quickly, his voice taking on a desperate pleading tone. Ignoring him, I shrugged out of his grip and quickly turned around before he could stop me.

I sincerely wished I hadn't.

A few cars down I saw Kane, his hair in that crazy disarray that I always loved. He was wearing a tight white T-shirt that defined his chest and firm arms perfectly, and some dark jeans. He looked sexy as always, and I instantly felt that pang of longing and desire burning in my veins, but before I could act on it, Kane threw his head back in laughter and shifted his body more towards me, revealing another person beside him.

None other than Kate.

The air left my lungs in a large, painful whoosh as I watched them both. She was smiling warmly up at him, saying something to which he nodded enthusiastically, a crooked grin on his face. I took a moment to drink in the sight of his face—his smile and the relaxed expression he held.

He seemed happy.

Before I knew it, Kane pulled Kate into his arms and gave her a tight hug, murmuring something over her shoulder, and what I saw in his eyes nearly forced the tears over my cheeks and the pain to ignite in my chest tenfold.

It was the look in his eyes I had wanted to see three weeks ago, the look which I had dreamed about countless nights. The look I prayed I would soon be able to witness.

But it wasn't with me that he got that look.

Because, as he carried on hugging Kate, his arms wrapped tightly around her shoulders, for the first time ever I saw Kane's eyes burning.

Burning with pure, warm, unadulterated . . . *Love.*

# 32. A Floodgate Finally Opens

## Kane

I felt . . . *Hopeless.*

And, as I sat there, in the pale decrepit lunchroom, I felt a bit angry, too, watching Suranne on the other side of the room talking with Lawrence. I know I should really be thanking him. He had, after all, been the one supporting her for the past three weeks.

Three weeks.

Christ, what was wrong with me?

It felt like the days had just whizzed past. Like it was only yesterday that Suranne had stood before me, her shoulders slumped and eyes defeated asking me to say those three important words to her that I just couldn't force out of my mouth.

But it wasn't. It was three goddamn weeks ago, and like the pussy that I am, I had left her alone, not calling, not texting, not talking to her at all.

But once nighttime came, it was a different story. I would drive past her house, lingering for a few moments. I would alternate between staring at my cell on my lap and up at her window, just telling myself to *call* her already. Tell her I love her, and then hopefully kiss those damn lips that I missed so much.

But I didn't.

Another thing I did as the days went on was think. A lot. Constantly questioning myself on the whys, whens, and wheres.

*Why* couldn't I just tell her? Did it mean that I didn't actually feel something for her after all?

*When* was it going to just . . . come to me? When was I going to have that life-changing epiphany when I nod and say the damn words out loud, knowing that I meant them?

And if it was going to happen, *where* would it be? Where would I take Suranne to tell her?

I could tell she was hurting, and it killed me to watch her every day hunched over defensively as if she were preparing for some attack. She just looked so weak, and knowing that, for some screwed up reason, there was nothing I could say or do drove me just about insane. I missed her like crazy; the littlest things would remind me of her. Of her laugh, or her smile, or the smell of her skin and hair, or the taste of her lips.

I gave a tight smile to Alex as he sat down with his tray of food, eyeing me curiously as to why I didn't have anything to eat. I shrugged in response. Eating was the last thing on my mind these days.

"So, you thought about this party tomorrow night? We need you back man . . . That shit'll be off the hook!" Alex crowed around his mouthfuls of food and I grimaced as bits of pizza flew out when he spoke.

"Jeez, can you *not* talk when you're eating? That shit is disgusting. I don't care to have some nasty-ass bit of cheese hit my face," I replied sharply, glaring at him for a second before returning my eyes to her.

She wasn't eating either. I could see Lawrence saying something to her and she shrugged in response.

"And no," I said, focusing back on Alex and his gross eating habits, "I'm not going to the damn party."

The last thing I needed were different bitches around me, all feeling up on my shit when I had already gone three weeks without any form of action. As much as I hated the thought of being with someone else other than my girl, I didn't wanna push my boundaries.

I'm still a man, and when under the influence of alcohol, having some chick's tight ass flaunted in front of you can just about make you forget all the other shit going on in your life.

It was bad enough how, since people had noticed Suranne and me no longer hanging around together, that shit had started going back to the way it used to be—chicks greeting me left, right, and center, giving me knowing looks and winks as they passed by. They might as well put signs on their chests saying "Do me."

Alex shrugged and followed the direction of my gaze, looking over his shoulder and focusing on Suranne. I heard him chuckle and as he looked back at me, his eyes alight with amusement.

"What?" I snapped, frowning at him and wondering what the hell he found so funny.

He held up his hands defensively and laughed again. "Nothin' man." With that he picked up his tray and left, calling out to a couple of blonde chicks and jogging after them. I watched him throw both his arms over their shoulders as they walked out and sighed, shaking my head before focusing back on her.

This had become my daily routine. Apart from the one lesson we had together every Friday, lunchtimes were the only time I could actually catch a glance of her. For some reason, I never managed to see her in the hallways anymore.

So every lunch period I just sat. Sat, and stared. Stared and longed. Longed and felt my chest restrict painfully. Got angry with myself, and eventually stormed off.

When I saw Lawrence lean closer and speak softly to her, a pang of jealousy and anger surged through every vein and artery in my body. My muscles seemed to stiffen and coil, ready to attack. But then, for the first time in the three weeks I'd been watching her trudge through the days, a smile formed on her lips, and a gentle laugh escaped her.

I immediately felt my face soften as I watched her; my body relaxed back into my chair as the sound of her subtle laughter caused warmth to ignite in me.

"Wow," I heard someone let out a slow whistle, "Why couldn't you love me like that?"

I snapped my head in the direction of the voice and cocked an eyebrow when I saw Kate standing there with an amused expression on her face.

"What do you mean by that?" I asked, shocked my question hadn't come out more sharply.

She smirked and pulled up the empty chair, twisting it around and straddling it backwards with her arms leaning on the back. "What I mean is," she started, pointing a finger at me, "the whole damn time you were with me, you *never* looked at me the way you just looked at her." She finished with a point over her shoulder. I followed the direction of her thumb and temporarily got lost in the vision of my girl. I sighed wistfully and focused back on Kate, and she laughed lightly.

"What the *hell* is so funny? You're the second person to laugh like that," I snapped at her, irritated that people seemed to be enjoying my misfortune.

Kate cocked an eyebrow at me and tilted her head slightly. "It's funny, *asshole*, because Kane Richards is in love."

I shook my head at her words; if I was in love then I'd be able to say the damn words already.

"I'm not in love," I mumbled, shifting my gaze back to Suranne. "If I were I'd tell her."

"So tell her," Kate shrugged simply, and I looked at her in shock.

"Don't you think I've *tried*? And why are you telling me this shit anyway? I thought you hated my ass."

She laughed. Again.

"Believe me, I do. But, this isn't about me, and, as much as people think I also hate Suranne, I really don't. I can *see* she loves you, just like I did. But there's a difference here, Kane," she sighed and rested her chin on her arms.

"Which *is*?"

"This time around, you actually love her back. I could see it in the way you looked at her, even if it was for like a second. I can still see it, and trust me, I know love when I see it," she replied calmly.

I returned my stare to Suranne. I felt that longing, that small, tiny bubble in my chest that was growing with every second and threatening to burst. But it wasn't like before; it was stronger, too powerful for me to handle and after a while, I had to look away, because that feeling scared the shit out of me.

All too soon I felt trapped, consumed, and completely ensnared by Suranne's presence. It was difficult to breathe. I shot out of my chair and rushed towards the exit not slowing my pace till I pushed open the double doors to the parking lot.

The cool air wrapped around me and freed the tingly tightening in my chest; its presence dissipated with every deep breath I took. I walked over to my car and leaned against the passenger door, holding my head in my hands and closing my eyes.

"You're frightened."

I jumped at the voice and snapped my head up.

"*Christ,* Kate, don't you ever give it a *rest?*" I sneered. I hated being snuck up on, and she knew that shit. She just smirked again and shook her head.

Bitch.

"You're frightened. That's why you won't tell her, and that's why, for some godforsaken reason, you just ran out of the cafeteria like a coward." She snickered and I glared at her, clenching my jaw.

"Go to hell," I spat defensively.

She shrugged and looked up at me, smiling. I didn't see any spitefulness in her green eyes, which shocked me. I only saw warmth.

"Why did I stay with you for all that time?" I muttered under my breath, shaking my head to myself.

She laughed and sighed. "Sometimes I wonder the same thing. But . . . I'd like to think we had some good times?" She looked up at me questioningly, a small smile on her lips.

I chuckled and nodded, "Yeah . . . that we did."

"Tell her, Kane." Her face abruptly became serious. "I waited for you to say it to me for years. Don't make her wait that long."

"When did you become . . . " I waved my hand at her, "this?"

"What?"

"This . . . understanding and all. I think I preferred you when you were showering me with hatred."

She laughed softly and sighed again. "I'm tired, Kane. It was three years ago. I just want to move on." She shrugged and smiled up at me before shifting her weight on her feet and fiddling with her hands. She took a deep breath and looked up, her eyes wide with remorse, and something close to regret.

"I'm sorry I left you the way I did. I should have been more understanding. I think I was just . . . too selfish at the time." She spoke softly, almost a whisper, and I just stood there gaping at her.

That was the first time she had ever apologized to me over our past relationship.

I told her it was alright, and just like that, the bitterness between us was gone. I thought I had gotten over all that bullshit, but it wasn't until she actually said those words that I felt it slip away. It was like a weight that I'd had no clue about had suddenly been lifted, leaving a calm, breezy peacefulness in its wake. We weren't quite friends, and I wasn't sure we ever would be, but it was OK. We just . . . were.

She filled me in on the past three years of her life, about her family, and her brother who I used to hate. I told her about Ashley, how she'd progressed and how, every once in a while she used to ask about her. Kate smiled a huge smile at that one, and asked me what I used to say.

"I told her I never cared, of course." I smirked at her, and she punched me in the arm. "Screw you," she muttered, but she was still smiling.

The bell rang signaling the end of class and the double doors burst open as every student rushed to get the hell out of there and begin their weekend. I noticed Lawrence come out and stand by his car; I clenched my jaw when I realized he was waiting for her.

And then there she was. I audibly let out a breath as soon as I saw her, that tiny tingly bubble growing inside me again. I saw her look around the lot and I wondered if she was looking for me. The bubble within me swelled at the thought, and the warmth that was surging through every fiber of my body was becoming almost too much to handle. I was panting, desperately trying to catch my breath and calm the hell down. Every time I tried to push it away, it just got stronger and stronger, the tingles turning into buzzing, humming electricity as I followed her every movement.

"What the hell is wrong with me?" I panted breathlessly, clutching my chest but unable to tear my eyes away from her.

"I *told* you. You *love* her," Kate murmured. Her words sunk into my brain and seeped into my veins; they rattled against my head and bounced on my tongue, just like they had when I was desperate to tell her before, but this time, my lips actually parted.

"*I love her,*" I blurted out breathlessly, my eyes still fixed on Suranne as her eyes darted around the lot everywhere but in my direction.

"I love her, I actually *love* her," I whispered in awe. I could feel myself grinning from ear to ear as I heard myself say the words out loud.

*Finally.*

"I know, who woulda thought, huh?" Kate replied dryly. "Kane Richards, pussy whipped." She shook her head in mock disbelief and I laughed loudly in response; my whole being felt light, almost weightless and carefree. I couldn't stop smiling and when I looked down at Kate, she was smiling along with me.

I grinned down at her and hugged her, because I was damn well sure that if she hadn't come up to me, if she hadn't laid herself out on the table and pushed me to understand, I wouldn't be standing here, with the huge grin on my damn face, feeling hopelessly in love.

She chuckled but hugged me back, squeezing me tightly.

"Thank you," I murmured over her shoulder, my heart racing and the bubble in my chest still threatening to burst, but this time I didn't care.

Because this time I knew I wasn't going to try and push it away. This time I was going to embrace it, and tell my girl that I loved her over and over again.

And this time, I knew that I would mean it.

## 33. WHO'S LOVING YOU

### Suranne

My brain hurt.

Along with every other part of my body. I swear my muscles were sore from crying. The image of Kane's face, so happy and elated and the love I saw in his eyes was constantly rewinding in my head. My eyes were so puffy that I could hardly see and I had the hiccups. *Great.* By the time evening came around, it had started to rain. Hard.

I lay on my bed, numb and exhausted, watching the rain smash against my window, blurring the glass into a dark, slimy mirage. Every inhalation brought pain, and exhalation left me aching.

As my room grew darker, the deathly red glow of my alarm clock brightened and burned the time in my peripheral vision: 7:05 p.m.

Without permission my mind wondered what *He* was doing. Images of him and that bloody crooked grin, his face alight with happiness and his eyes burning . . . Burning with that look as he wrapped his arms around Kate.

Was he with her?

I closed my eyes tightly, shaking my head against the scratchy material of my pillow, and tried to think of something else.

A knock on my bedroom door startled me, and I jumped, coughing out a raspy greeting. It was my aunt, of course.

She glanced at me, trying not to stare at the pitiful mess I had become and cautiously treaded into my room, placing herself at the end of my bed.

"Joe called," she murmured, her voice temporarily drowning out the constant pounding of the rain.

I nodded in response. Joe was her partner/boss, and I knew that whenever he called, it basically meant an evening on my own whilst my aunt went to the office. I had a growing suspicion that they were doing more than just working, but she wasn't sharing any info.

"I'm not sure I want to leave you alone the entire night, but it would seem silly for me to make the long journey back home in the middle of the night just to go back to work in the morning." She seemed nervous, almost worried as to whether her excuse was plausible. I couldn't help the small smile as I continued staring at the window.

"It's OK. I'll be fine. Promise." I sighed and closed my eyes, grimacing at the burning sensation behind my eyelids.

"Honey, I don't know what's going on right now, but I'm worried. I need to know if you are really going to be OK."

I turned my head to face her and opened my eyes, only to be met with the same blue-grey eyes that my mum had. The resemblance was almost calming, as if I could see my mum through her, and her loving concern made me give a teary smile. A part of me was sad at being truly alone for tonight, but I couldn't keep her here just to comfort me.

"I'll be OK, I promise," I reassured her, and she nodded, taking my hand and giving it a gentle squeeze.

"I made some chicken pasta for you. It's in the oven. I *want* it *eaten*, Suranne. You hear me?" I nodded and smiled as she lifted herself from my bed and slipped out. I continued to sit, staring at the window as the constant drum of the rain carried through my ears. After a few minutes I heard the front door close, followed by the gentle thrum of my aunt's car. The tyres scratched against the gravel and the sound of the engine carried off into the distance then disappeared altogether.

Silence.

It was silent. And I was alone.

I took a deep, painful breath, then let it out in a long aching exhale. I got up from my bed and put my hair up in a messy bun, deciding to have a shower. I walked into the hallway and grabbed a towel from the airing cupboard, revelling in its fluffy warmth before padding back towards my room.

Just before I closed the bathroom door I could have sworn I heard a car pull up my drive, but I took no notice, shaking my head and thinking it was my imagination. I placed the towel on the side and reached to turn on the shower but stopped when a gentle tapping resounded from downstairs. I frowned, going completely still and listening again. If it was my aunt she could just let herself in, unless she'd forgotten her keys.

The tapping started again, louder this time and I left the bathroom, trudging down the stairs convinced that she had forgotten her keys. With a sigh, I opened the door only to be greeted by the person I least expected.

Kane stood outside my porch, the rain beating down on him vigorously, his sweatshirt clinging to every muscle and dent on his chest, his hair glistening with raindrops, his eyes dark and deep, boring into mine with such an intensity my knees felt weak.

"Kane," I breathed, my voice thick with surprise "W—what are you . . . ?" I couldn't finish the sentence. I was too breathless.

He ran his hand through his dripping hair and sighed, a few raindrops falling off his thick red lips.

"I can't . . . we both know that whenever I speak, I just . . . mess it up, so . . ." his voice was low and deep and I revelled in the sound that had been missing from my ears for so long. Too long.

I couldn't speak yet. I could hardly breathe, and my eyes were impossibly wide, greedily drinking in the exquisite sight of a wet Kane Richards. I could almost feel his warmth, and my body was shrieking to be touched by him, my heart hammering in my chest.

I was still speechless and he sighed again, fumbling in his jeans pocket for something whilst muttering a few curses under his breath.

"Just . . . I just, was wondering . . . I know I need to . . . *Damn*," he said exasperated at himself. I couldn't help but breathe a laugh at his discomfort. He snapped his head up to look at me, and I saw his face relax and his eyes warm as he listened to my light chuckle before he blinked and seemed to focus again.

"Umm . . . I know that, uh . . ." He sighed and shook his head, thrusting a crumpled, sopping wet card in my hands. I turned it over and read the smudged address on it, frowning in confusion.

"Suranne," Kane murmured, stepping closer as rain contin- ued to drop from his hair and lips. He brought his shaky hands up to cup my face and a sigh escaped my lips at his touch. My eyes closed briefly, not ever wanting him to leave. His scent, coupled with the steam from the rain, swirled around me and took the breath from my lungs.

"Meet me here," he breathed gently, his face a few inches from mine. "Please? Just . . . meet me here, tonight."

I opened my eyes and glanced down at the dripping card but didn't recognise the address. I sighed and closed my eyes again. It seemed that I was always following Kane wherever he wanted me to; I was always going to him.

I knew I always would.

"OK," I whispered and I heard him breathe out a huge sigh of relief.

"Really?" he asked, his eyes wide with excitement, a lopsided grin on his face.

I nodded and gave a weak smile in return.

"Thank you," he breathed and closed his eyes before turning away and jogging back to his car. I watched him drive off in disbelief. Now that his presence was gone I couldn't help but feel angry. Angry that I had agreed to see him so quickly and hadn't asked him about Kate. Angry that whenever I was around him my body reacted in crazy and frightening ways.

Angry that, even though I was *angry*, I was going to meet him, regardless.

I frowned down at the card; he hadn't told me when to meet him, but I smiled when I saw a faded and smudged *9 p.m.* written in blue ink on the back.

I took a deep breath and turned around, closing the door.

I really needed that shower.

\*\*\*

I clasped my hands tightly together as I sat in the back of the taxi; my nerves were taut, stretched as far as they would go. I was frustrated that Kane hadn't given me any details. I didn't know whether to dress casual or smart, so I'd opted for a mixture of both. I was wearing black trousers and a white button down-shirt that reached midthigh, and a thick, black fitted belt at the waist. I put my hair up but left a few strands curled around my shoulder and neck and wore simple hoop earrings and minimal makeup.

I watched the traffic through the window until it became a blurry mixture of colours and as we pulled up to the building, my heart beat wildly in my chest.

The building was . . . *Huge.*

I wondered if it was a hotel of some sort; if so, it must be one of those really flashy ones with eighteen floors and exquisite furniture.

I paid and thanked the taxi driver, walked into the building, and stood in the foyer uncomfortably. As I busily drank in my surroundings, I heard a throat clearing behind me and turned around to the intoxication of Kane's cologne. It wrapped around me and sank in deeply as I breathed. I let my gaze drift over him and felt my body react instantly. His upper body was leaning against the wall, he was holding a black suit jacket over his shoulder with one hand, and his other was in his dark jeans pocket. He was wearing a crisp white button-down shirt. *And was that a black tie hanging loosely around his neck?* His hair was neatly spiked at the front and he had his usual stud earring in his ear.

Words seriously couldn't describe how good he looked at that moment in time.

"Hey," I breathed weakly, my eyes still roaming over his ridiculously magnetic form. Kane gave a warm smile, and pushed himself off the wall, walking slowly towards me. He moved a loose curl that was on my neck behind my ear and focused deeply on my face.

"Hey," he replied, his eyes bright with contained excitement. "Come with me."

He grabbed my hand and led me to a large arched doorway with ornate carvings on the arch and around the edges of the doors.

"We've missed dinner, but we can always get some after. But this . . ." he trailed off and pushed open the door. I gasped in response.

It was a hall of some kind, with dimmed lights and jazz music filling the room, played by a band situated on a large stage. The walls were a gentle shade of red and to the right were various round tables, their white linen cloths glowing from the single candles situated in the center of each one. A few people were seated at the tables, laughing and interacting with each other.

But the main event was happening in the middle of the hall. Couples were dancing, seemingly consumed by the soft music that echoed off the walls and trilled into their ears.

I looked up at Kane with an expression of utter disbelief. He gave me the crooked grin and I felt myself shudder in response.

"What is this place?" I asked quietly as my eyes followed the people mingling and swaying on the dance floor.

"The building itself," Kane started whilst moving me forward with his hand on the small of my back, "is my father's." I saw him nod his head to a few people as we walked past. I smiled at them politely.

"And this . . . " He gestured to the dance floor, "this is the annual ball. It used to be held in November on my dad's request, but when he died, they changed it to the end of April, in remembrance of his death."

I felt my jaw go slack at his words, shocked and a little bit touched that so many people would attend an event in remembrance of someone. I suppose it made sense, if this was Kane's father's building. These people must have been his colleagues.

Kane looked down at me and gave me a sad smile. "We used to go every year when my Dad was alive, but when he died, we just . . . couldn't. This is the first time I've been here in three years." He sighed and shook his head regretfully. "He was a great guy."

I smiled up at him warmly and lightly touched his arm. "I wish I could have met him. From the looks of it, he was very popular," I said, once again looking around at the hall filled with laughter and gentle music.

Kane chuckled and nodded at me. "He was too popular for his own good. He had chicks digging him from left, right, and centre," he laughed.

"Like father, like son," I muttered dryly as Kane led me to the middle of the hall. I felt myself grimace as images of him hugging Kate came back to me. Kane sighed and looked down at me.

"Yeah . . . you're right. Like father, like son," he confirmed and I glared at him, not finding his comment funny, but he just smirked and wrapped his arms around my waist. "Because," he ducked his head down to whisper in my ear, "although he had women wanting him from every direction, his heart belonged to someone else completely, Suranne. And that someone for me . . . is you."

He unbuttoned my coat and pushed it off my shoulders and I gazed up at him breathlessly. I saw his eyes darken as my skintight shirt was exposed, and he threw the coat, along with his suit jacket, on the nearest chair, then wrapped his arms tightly around my waist.

My head was spinning from confusion, but as I started to question him, the music died down and the main singer grabbed the mic.

"Good evening, ladies and gentlemen. Once again, welcome to the Daniel Richards Thirteenth Annual Ball. We suggest you grab ahold of that one person you love right now and don't let them go throughout the duration of our next song. Hope you enjoy and we wish you a great evening."

I looked up at Kane and smiled as the song started playing through the large speakers. I watched as his chocolate-brown eyes glimmered in the dimmed lights and candles as he gazed warmly down at me. He held on to me more tightly and kissed my forehead, whispering there, "Listen to the lyrics, Suranne."

As the introduction to the song wound down, the man standing on the stage started singing deeply into the mic:

"*When I . . . Had you, I treated you bad, and wrong, my dear.*"

The backup singers harmonised his words, along with the bass player, and I closed my eyes as Kane started to sway us gently to the song, which I recognised.

"*And girl, since . . . Since you've went away, don't you know I . . Sit around . . . With my head, hanging down, and I wonder . . . Who's loving you,*"

I rested my head against his chest and he placed his chin atop of it as we swayed softly from side to side. I felt lost to the music, completely blocking out the other couples filling the hall around us. My chest constricted painfully as the song carried on:

"*I . . . I . . . I . . . I should have never . . . ever . . . ever made you cry, and girl since . . . Since you've been gone, don't you know I . . . sit around, with my head . . . hanging down. And I wonder . . . Who's loving you.*

"*Life without love, ha . . . It's ooh, so lonely . . . I don't think, I don't think I'm gonna make it. All my life, all my life, yeah, I've been lost to you only . . .*

"*Come on and take it, girl . . .*

*Come on and take it girl, because all, All I can do... All I can do, since you've been gone, is cry.*" I felt myself laugh softly and looked up at Kane questioningly, to which he smirked as his eyes burned into mine

"Alright, I didn't cry, but I was close," Kane murmured through his smile and I giggled softly, shaking my head at him as we continued to move gently. The song wove itself back to the chorus and I sighed, staring up at Kane, completely lost in the burning force of his gaze. I watched him take a deep breath and close his eyes before he leaned down and rested his forehead against mine.

And then he opened his eyes.

And it was there.

I felt the pressure in my chest expand as my heart did a double take. I let out a raspy breath as my eyes locked with his.

His eyes blazed and swirled with the one thing I had been desperate for over these past weeks. They blazed with *love.*

I smiled up at him, and a happy, relieved sob escaped my chest. Kane smiled back and lifted his hand to brush away the tears that now slid down my cheeks.

"Suranne . . . " he whispered softly, his eyes piercing right through me into the depths of my heart.

"*I love you.*"

The words pushed me off the edge and I closed my eyes and locked my arms around his neck, my tears sinking into his fresh white shirt. The song wound down to an end as Kane wrapped his arms tightly around my waist and crushed me to him.

"I love you, too," I choked into his shoulder, feeling his chest rumble as he chuckled into my ear.

***

I sighed contently, leaning back against Kane's chest. We were sitting at one of the tables in the corner of the hall. He had lined two chairs up and propped his back up against one whilst his legs rested on the other and I sat on his lap. The music continued to pulse through the room and the dance floor was crowded. I watched as couples twirled and swayed whilst Kane played with my hair softly.

"Kane?" Throughout all of this, there was one thing that had still been bothering me.

"Mmm?" He brought his head down and pressed his lips to my temple softly. I swallowed heavily, "Why were you hugging Kate in the parking lot today?" I blurted and held my breath, waiting for his answer.

"To say thank you," he replied simply as he nuzzled my neck and I resisted the urge to moan as his tongue darted out against my skin.

"Why?" I asked breathlessly, my mind becoming incoherent as he continued his assault.

"She forced me to realise the truth, Suranne. If it weren't for her pushing me to admit that it was only fear stopping me from coming to you, I still wouldn't be here."

I sighed in relief and melted against his chest as he carried on kissing down my neck. He started slowly brushing his hands along my arms and this time I couldn't contain the shiver that rippled through me at the feel of his touch. Again.

I squirmed against his lap and smirked when I felt a certain something straining against my lower back. Kane groaned and bit my ear lobe.

"You know, I think *all* of me missed you," he whispered hoarsely, his words causing desire to shoot through my body. "I can see that," I murmured as his hands gripped my hips and pushed me back against him. "Maybe you should take me home." Kane stopped his movements and I turned around in his lap only to see a frown and a hurt expression on his face.

"You wanna go home?" he asked softly, and I realised that he thought I wanted to go home alone.

I leaned forward and gripped his tie, using it to pull him towards me, "Well of course I wanna go home," I smirked as confusion crossed his face.

"My aunt's away and I do believe you've got three weeks to make up for." I tilted my head and smiled sweetly at him as understanding and lust flashed in his eyes. He grabbed my face and pushed his lips against mine, kissing me passionately before I pulled away.

"Take me home Kane," I gasped. "Now."

He grinned and kissed me chastely on the lips.

"Did I tell you that I love you?"

# 34. A Fire Reignited

## Kane

"Damn, Suranne," I hissed, fighting the urge to close my eyes.

We were in my car; I was driving as quickly as possible without getting us killed. She was leaning over the console kissing my neck, and she had just placed her hand over my crotch.

I needed to get her home. Fast.

I groaned and gripped the steering wheel more tightly as her hand made a small circling motion. If she kept this up I'd be having her in the damn car.

"I need you so bad, Kane," I heard her whimper and . . . Christ. After three weeks of having no action whatsoever, then suddenly having, well, *this*, I was seriously about to lose it.

"*Jesus*," I muttered, because she couldn't just say that to me right now. "You can't *say* that to me right now, baby. Christ, I'm half tempted to just pull the hell over and put the back seats down."

She breathed a husky giggle right in my ear and I groaned again, pushing my foot down a bit further, because damn, why weren't we there already?

I breathed a sigh of relief once we reached her drive, but with the state I was in, it came out more like a rough grunt, and Suranne just chuckled in my ear again. I threw open my door and jogged around to her side, opening her door and grabbing her hand, snatching her out of the car. I shut the door and pushed her up against it. Hard.

My mouth instantly connected with her neck and I groaned again, because it had been too long since I last tasted her skin. I carried on licking and nipping her skin lightly as her breathing became labored and choppy. Two can play that game.

Cupping her face in my hands I kissed her with all the feeling I could muster. At a time like this I should really be gentle and soft, doing the whole 'making love' thing, but right now, I was too excited for slow and gentle.

I needed to feel her. Now.

She tentatively caressed my tongue with her own, sweeping it silkily around mine, and I reveled in her sweet taste. Everything about her drove me crazy. I pulled away and gazed into her wide gray eyes that shone with fiery lust. Her cheeks were tinted a soft pink and her lips were parted and full and just made me want to kiss her all the damn time. I brushed my lips against hers, softly feeling the intense feelings in my chest bubble and churn, just like they had when I was in the parking lot today and when I was dancing with her tonight.

As the bubble in my chest rose intensely, I felt the unspoken words flashing in my head, twisting around my tongue. It was like there was nothing I could do to stop them. I didn't *want* to stop them.

"I love you," I breathed against her lips, trailing them along her jaw and down the creamy tight skin of her neck and over her collarbone.

"I love you, too," she gasped, her head thrown back and her heavy breathing pushing her chest against mine. I groaned at hearing her say the words and was shocked how they only turned me on even more.

She grabbed my hand and pushed my mouth away, dragging me toward her front door as she fumbled around feverishly for her keys. I smirked at her hurried movements and softly took the keys from her, kissing her gently on the lips once. I successfully opened the door and gestured with my hand for her to enter first. She smiled warmly and walked past, her delicious, sultry scent wafting up at me.

I slammed the door shut, my eyes fixed to the back of Suranne's figure with a predatory leer. She jumped and whirled around at the sound of the door slamming, but didn't have a chance to respond before I grabbed her waist and smashed my lips to hers, pushing her backwards at the same time until we both collapsed onto the couch, me on top, kissing her frenziedly. She whimpered against my lips and spread her legs allowing me to rest in between her thighs. Her heat was burning through my jeans, driving me crazy.

"Suranne," I panted through my kisses on her lips and jaw, "I don't . . *know* if I can be *slow*." I breathed against her, watching as her eyes closed and she breathed out a silent moan.

"I don't want you slow," she whispered, her eyes still closed and her breathing heavy.

I continued kissing down her neck, occasionally smirking arrogantly at her mewls and soft pleads for me. Reluctantly, I sat up on my knees and the look of her eyes, wide and lustful, her full pink lips, and her soft tongue darting out briefly and wetting her lower lip, leaving it glistening and red, would be burned into my mind forever.

But as much as the horny animal within me just wanted to ravish her right then on her aunt's sofa, the other part, the gentle Kane Richards part, wanted to lay her down on her bed, watch as her hair flared softly on her pillows, and kiss every inch of her skin lovingly.

That part of me wanted to worship her.

And as I gazed down at her, the animal within me got pushed aside, and that gentle Kane Richards part of me won over.

I ran my hand down her arm and linked my fingers through hers, smiling down at her warmly.

"Come on baby, let's go upstairs," I murmured, leaning down and kissing her lips softly. She sighed, and returned my kiss before I pulled away and unwound her legs from my waist with a devious grin.

She ducked her head with a sheepish smile, but I wasn't having any of that. I placed my fingers under her chin and pushed her face up to look at me, leaning down once again to kiss her gently, this time sweeping my tongue against her top lip, tasting her sweet skin. The moment a gentle moan escaped her throat I broke away.

Because seriously, I needed to get to a bed before I became a victim of self-combustion.

I tugged her off the couch and just as I was about to lead the way, I saw something familiar flicker in her eyes. It was a look I thoroughly enjoyed.

It was a look that was nothing but pure, one hundred percent Suranne, the I-want-you-so-bad seducing vixen.

She placed a hand on my chest and pushed, smirking as she walked past me and shrugged out of her coat, giving me a look over her shoulder as her hips sashayed from side to side while she walked towards the stairs, now being the one to lead me.

I stood, my eyes watching her ass as she walked up the stairs, enjoying the view far too much to even move.

"Don't make me wait, *Richards*," Suranne called at me from the top of the stairs.

I took those stairs two at a time and then I kissed her and pulled her against my hips roughly. I was back, full swing.

I grabbed her hand and tugged her towards her room, pushing her door open swiftly with my other hand, not caring about how it banged and rebounded against the wall. I pulled her in front of me and wrapped my arms around her waist, kissing her softly as I backed her up against the bed, until her legs reached the edge. I continued pushing, gently falling on top of her but still not breaking away from her lips. She snaked her hand up my chest and her little hands fisted into my hair, tugging hard and making me groan against her mouth.

I pushed away from her to undo the knot in my tie but her hand flashed out and grabbed my wrist, halting my movements.

"No," she panted with a sly smile, "the tie stays on."

I smirked, admiring her control.

Her fingers ran smoothly down my shirt, her eyes following her movements as she began slowly to undo the buttons on my shirt. Once she finished, she paused, as if memorizing the image before she pushed the shirt off my shoulders, leaving it in a creased white heap behind me. I heard her let out a small whimper as she ran her fingers over the muscles of my chest and abdomen, her eyes hooded with lust and her breathing increasingly labored and heavy.

I ran my hands up her arms, over her shoulders and across the collarbones visible beneath the button-down shirt that made her body look so amazing. I groaned as I unbuttoned the first two buttons and the top of her chest came into view, straining against the confines of her sheer black bra.

"So sexy," I breathed silently, more to myself than to her as I continued unclipping her belt and unbuttoning the rest of her shirt. I pushed it off her shoulders and she lifted her torso, allowing me to pull it off her completely. I tossed it somewhere behind me.

The next few minutes were spent shedding each other's clothes. The sounds of the various garments filling the floor surrounded us, along with our heavy breaths and moans of appreciation whenever a new body part was revealed. The temperature around us rose perceptibly and I brushed a bead of sweat from her neck before brushing my lips across the same spot, continuing a trail of kisses down, across her chest, kissing the sensitive skin as her whimpers of my name grew louder.

I positioned myself between her thighs and sat up, wrapping her legs around my waist.

She let out a frustrated sigh and wrapped my tie around her wrist, jerking me towards her roughly. My lips brushed against hers as she whispered to me in a husky voice.

"I want you, Kane."

I groaned and thrust my tongue into her mouth. And without any hesitance, I gave her what we both wanted.

The heat and the anticipation of finally feeling her caused my body to shudder and she let out a sexy groan. Willing me to move against her, she lifted her hips, causing me to gasp into her neck.

*Control*, Kane . . . *control.*

Her heavy breaths were in my ear; her sweet scent, mingled with the faint musk of her sweat, was turning my mind hazy.

I took a deep breath and lifted my head, looking at her face to distract me. Her gray eyes burned into mine with desire and passion. But as I continued staring at her, I felt them flicker and blaze with the love she felt for me and I smiled at her, sighing before kissing her lips softly and continuing.

The air was thick and hot and I could feel the pleasure inside me building and building, reaching a new level. Moaning my name, she arched her back and shuddered, driving me over the edge. I exhaled a shaky breath against her neck as the pleasuring tingles shot through my body. I would never get over how good she felt. Nothing compared to that.

A tranquil calm washed over me as I gained control of my breathing and lay beside her. I tucked my arm beneath her still-trembling body and pulled her against my chest. Her hand drew lazy circles against my skin as I closed my eyes and rubbed her back, stroking her hair softly.

I heard her breathe a quiet laugh that sounded so calm and carefree that I found myself smiling down at her.

"What's so funny?" I asked her, my voice tired and low.

She chuckled, her hot breath tickling my skin. "When I told my aunt that I would be fine before she left, I didn't think I'd be *this* fine."

I laughed and pressed my lips against the top of her head, before smirking as I was reminded of something.

I rolled us over so I was on top, my smirk still plastered on my face.

"So, you like my tie, huh?"

Her face filled with a light shade of pink and I couldn't help but chuckle at her all-of-a sudden coyness.

"Yeah," she replied shyly, looking up at me through her eyelashes. That just made my body twitch in response.

I leaned down to slowly kiss her lips, nipping at the skin lightly as she fisted her hands in my hair and deepened the kiss with her tongue. She squirmed underneath me and sighed against my mouth softly. I pulled away and kissed her cheeks and chin chastely as she ran her hands over my chest, smiling whenever her fingers brushed over the loose black tie around my neck.

I stroked her cheek and down her neck continuing over her shoulders as she gazed up at me lovingly, her eyes flickered to my mouth before returning to my face. I chuckled and shook my head, because reading her was so easy these days.

And right now my girl wanted my lips on hers.

I leaned down and kissed her again, before a loud vibrating filled the room and shocked us apart. I looked around the room before spotting her cell phone on her side table, moving across the surface. I distractedly picked it up and glanced at the number, but the area code was unfamiliar and so I tossed it to the ground with a shrug.

"Kane! I should answer it," she scolded, her tone disapproving. I shrugged again and began kissing down her neck, ignoring her words.

"Kane," she sighed, trying to escape my grip but I tightened my hold on her.

The vibration stopped and I lifted my head, smiling down at her in victory. She rolled her eyes and shook her head at me. "Why can't I ever say no to you?" she sighed.

I smirked arrogantly, "'Cause you can't resist me."

She frowned up at me, "I know, and it only means you'll get away with murder," she muttered.

I grinned and shook my head against her lips, "I won't murder you."

I heard her giggle as I kissed her top lip, shifting myself between her legs again, but that damn vibration started up once more and she stopped, turning her head to the noise of her cell phone.

"Kane . . . I should answer it," she murmured to me softly, but I shook my head and lifted myself on my arms.

"No," I replied, kissing her lips softly as I positioned myself against her. I pulled away and grinned crookedly. "You can answer it after another round."

And just like that, we started all over again . . .

## 35. Reality Comes Crashing Back

### Suzanne

I smiled as his hard chest pressed against mine, his deep heavy breathing matching my own, and he buried his face in my neck, occasionally pressing light kisses to the skin there. I lifted my hand and ran it through his hair softly, relishing the smooth locks. His breathing calmed down as I continued stroking his hair.

"You have to leave soon," I sighed. "As much as I like having you here, my aunt will be back soon, and I don't think I can handle anymore action." I winced as I shifted my body beneath him, feeling the ache spread through my limbs. It was a good ache, an ache that screamed *Kane Richards*.

But it was an ache, nonetheless.

Kane rolled to his side, propping his head up with his hand. "To be fair, you instigated that last one," he replied, with a quirk of his brow.

"True," I nodded and leaned over to kiss his lips gently.

"So . . . your aunt and her boss, huh?" Kane mused as he lifted his other hand and rested it on my hip, his thumb rubbing small circles on the skin.

I shrugged. "Yeah . . . I don't know anything for certain, but I'm pretty sure they're mixing business with pleasure," I mumbled.

When Kane didn't reply I looked up at him and smirked when I saw his eyes suddenly lust over. He leaned over so he could whisper huskily in my ear, and I couldn't help but giggle at his suggestive words for more.

"Well, I dunno about you, but I'm hungry. It seems you've drained me of energy," I teased and his only reply was a slap to my backside as I went to get dressed.

***

"So, you'll come over later today, right? I mean Ashley says she misses the shit out of you."

It was 3 a.m. and Kane stood outside my door, his arm resting against the doorframe above my head and his body leaning over me. I was trailing my fingers over his white shirt, occasionally tugging the black tie. I couldn't help myself; there was just something about it that looked so sexy on him.

I laughed and raised an eyebrow, to which he smiled back seemingly deep in thought. After a long pause, he replied, "OK, so she didn't say the whole 'shit' thing, but whatever, she misses you regardless. You get my point. So what ya say? You coming?" His soft voice carried over to my ears and I shivered as I gazed into his large, pleading, chocolate-brown eyes.

"Please come," he whispered against my lips, and I hesitated, not sure whether I'd be able to face going inside his house again. The last time I was in his room, it was filled with anger and pain, as I had witnessed a different side to Kane.

He seemed to understand my hesitancy, and he sighed softly, his face twisting in remorse.

"We won't have to go into my room," he promised firmly. "We can just hang out downstairs. Y'know, with Ashley and Mom."

His voice caused a tightening in my chest. I had never heard him sound so vulnerable, apart from when he was talking about how his father died, that day at the park.

Kane really was ashamed of his behaviour that night. I could see it on his face when his eyes met mine and then darted to his feet.

"It's fine," I whispered back, because I loved him, and now knew that he felt the same way. I would walk through hell and back just to see him smile.

His head snapped up, and his eyes were wide with hope. "Really?" he asked, shocked that I had agreed.

I smiled and nodded my head. "Of course. I miss your sister, too. And I love going to your house. You know that."

His face abruptly relaxed into relief, and the smile that I had wanted to see on his lips finally came into view. He brought his hands up to cup my face as he kissed my lips several times.

"I love you," he sighed as his eyes closed and he remained smiling.

I would never tire of those words leaving his lips. Ever.

"I love you, too," I grinned, feeling a deep warmth spread through me.

Reluctantly he pulled away, looking at his car over his shoulder. "I should probably go," he frowned. "But I'll be back to pick you up later." He seemed to be reassuring both of us. I nodded and forced a smile, not wanting him to leave, but he had no choice.

His frown deepened, and his lips formed an adorable reluctant pout. "I kinda . . . don't want to," he muttered sourly, seemingly confused at this fact. I laughed and leaned up on my tiptoes, pressing my lips against his.

"That's what happens when you love someone . . . *baby*." He narrowed his eyes playfully at me. "Whatever." He shrugged nonchalantly. "I'll be cool without you for a few hours."

"Mmmhmm," I replied, my voice sceptical.

"I'll probably have stuff to do anyway." His voice remained casual, and yet he still made no move towards his car. I tried to fight the smile from my face.

"Yeah, me too," I said, imitating his casual tone. At my words his eyes snapped to mine.

"Like *what*?" he demanded. I once again fought off the grin that was threatening to spread over my face.

"Oh, y'know . . ." I trailed off, eager to hear his response. I could see the curiosity in his eyes and something close to *jealousy*.

"Well *no*, I don't know, which is *why* I'm asking you to explain for me," he replied sarcastically. I couldn't contain it any longer; I broke out into a huge grin and chuckled, shaking my head.

"What's so damn funny?"

I continued chuckling at his petulant face. Sometimes he was too cute. "I'm just messing with you," I teased, pushing his chest playfully. He rolled his eyes but I saw his lips twitching up into a smile. After a few seconds he shook his head.

"Whatever," he said and leaned down, wrapping his arms around me and enveloping me in a tight hug. "Imma miss you," he murmured into my ear, and I nodded, telling him that I would miss him as well.

He squeezed me gently then let go, placed a final kiss on my lips, and walked to his car. I watched him get in and rest his head against the steering wheel for a few seconds. His lips appeared to be moving, as if muttering to himself, and then he started the car and drove off without a backward glance.

I sighed and walked inside, locking the door behind me. Too tired to do anything downstairs, I made my way up the stairs. I heard a distinct vibrating coming from my room, but didn't have the energy to run for it, and so I continued lazily making my way up each step.

I pushed open my door, my eyes burning along with the whole of my body, screaming for rest and, with sleep at the forefront of my mind; I collapsed on my bed, falling asleep within seconds. My last thought being that I'd forgotten to check who had rung me in the first place.

The slam of the front door and my aunt's voice trilling from the kitchen woke me up. I groggily looked at my alarm clock, and was shocked to see that it was in the afternoon.

I guess that's what Kane does to you, I thought to myself wryly, shaking my head and getting up to sit at the edge of my bed sleepily.

"Suranne? You up, honey?"

"Yeah." I winced at how cracked and dry my voice sounded. I decided to have a shower, and grabbed some fresh clothes and a towel, telling my aunt that I would be down shortly.

Contentment set in as the hot water cascaded over my skin and melted away the soreness of my joints. After spending a good half hour cleaning up and just enjoying the water beating down on me, I stepped out and dried off, brushing my teeth and blow drying my hair. As soon as the hair dryer shut off, I once again heard the vibrating of my phone. I dashed out of the bathroom and grabbed it, flipping it open just in time, without even looking at the screen.

"Hello?" I breathed faintly, out of breath.

"Hey baby!"

"*Mum?*"

The voice on the phone didn't wait for my reply, it just carried on speaking.

"Time to come home, honey, Mummy's back and she missed you!"

Dread coursed through my veins and my heart sped up rapidly, beating its protest.

And just like that, reality came crashing down onto me with a force that left me breathless and on my knees.

My mum was back.

It was time for me to leave?

# 36. Agonising Orders

## Suranne

The tears carried on rolling down my cheeks as I heard my mum explain why it was necessary for me to come home. She was sick. Her trip had been about getting treatment for some illness I didn't even *know* about.

"Mum," I sobbed, interrupting her, "I'm just not *ready* to come home yet. *Please*." My voice choked on the last sentence as my chest tightened painfully, leaving me gasping for air.

"Suranne," my mum sighed over the phone, "I've already reenrolled you in school and booked your return flight, darling. I'm doing a little better, but I really do want you near me."

My chest heaved uncontrollably at her words. She sounded weak and tired. Anger and guilt surged through me. I sniffed, wishing for Kane's arms around me right now.

"I'm sorry, Mum. When's my flight?"

"It takes off at 6 p.m. your time, today."

"*Today*?!" I gasped. I couldn't leave *today*. She couldn't make me leave *today*.

"Afraid so, honey. I've been trying to reach you since yesterday. I'm sure it's a shock, but you *knew* this was a temporary arrangement." Her voice became softer towards the end and I felt my chest tighten once again.

I pulled the phone away from my ears and glanced at the time.

3:10 p.m.

I had less than three hours to get packed and leave.

*Leave.*

247

# 37. UNREPAIRABLE PAIN

## Kane

I sighed and flipped my cell shut, irritated that I'd missed Surrane's call. This was the third time I had tried to call her back, only for it to go straight to voice mail. I mean, who the hell was she on the damn phone to?

A small tapping on my bedroom door pulled me from my frustration and I smiled, knowing it was Ashley.

"What up?" I called out. She pushed the door open and bounced inside, her ponytail bobbing with every step and a beaming smile lighting up her face.

"What time are you getting Suranne?" she asked, her wide brown eyes shining brightly with excitement. It had been weeks since Ashley had seen her, and she missed her like crazy.

I chuckled and mussed her hair up, knowing she hated it, and she whined and slapped my hand outta the way with a huff.

"I'm trying to call her now but she's still on the phone. But as soon as I get hold of her I'll tell her I'm on my way, 'K?"

Ashley grinned and nodded her head energetically before skipping out of my room. As I watched her leave, she smacked into my mom, who had just appeared in the doorway. I rolled my eyes and laughed.

"Why is everyone hounding me today? Christ I'll just leave my door open to the whole world," I teased as they both stood smiling in my doorway.

"Will your girlfriend be staying for dinner?" Mom asked, her voice emphasizing the word *girlfriend* with a smirk as if it was the most uncommon thing in the damn world.

Well, I guess for me it kind of was.

I chuckled but then frowned, reaching for my cell and trying to ring her once again.

"I don't know," I muttered while pressing the send button. Once again, her voice mail responded and I couldn't help the irritation that flared within me. Whoever the hell she was on the phone with, she needed to end the damn call already, because I was getting impatient.

"Maybe you should just surprise her," Ashley suggested, with a shrug and a hopeful smile. I sighed and glanced at the time on my cell.

3:40 p.m.

"Yeah, I'll uh . . . go at four or some shit, I mean thing," I mumbled, catching myself. I could at least follow my dad's wishes in front of Ashley. I fiddled with the remote for my TV hoping I'd be able to catch the last twenty minutes of the game. Mom ushered Ashley out of my room and closed the door. I heard Ashley laugh as their voices carried on down the stairs and couldn't help but smile at the sound. My sister laughed a lot now and, after the constant tears months ago, it was a noise I would never take for granted again.

I watched the game with unseeing eyes, finding it difficult to concentrate on the moving figures swirling across the screen and the monotone commentary that filled my ears. I was anxious for her arms, her scent, and her lips. Her body.

I didn't realize how difficult it would be to separate from her; even if it was only for a couple of hours. It felt like instinct to just want to be around her, and pulling, walking, or driving away was an action that threatened my damn survival. Right now my body was drawn tight, my head and limbs feeling jittery as a cold, uneasy shiver rippled down my spine. I frowned at my uneasiness, but rationalized that I had just been away from her longer than I could handle. With a last glance at the clock, I made the decision to go pick her up unannounced. It's not like she didn't know she was coming over today anyway.

I pulled on my jacket hurriedly, darting down the stairs and into the kitchen where Mom was cooking dinner. I smiled and kissed the top of her head softly.

"Smells good," I murmured into her hair and she turned; a small smile on her lips as she reached up and kissed my cheek briefly. My heart warmed when I smelled mint on her breath, instead of the rancid sour alcohol that I had become used to.

"I'm proud of you, Mom." I hugged her to me tightly and she laughed into my chest, the noise calm and content. Giving her a squeeze, I told her I was going to go pick up Suranne and she released me, nodding her head.

I called out a hasty *bye* to Ashley and jogged to my car, eager to see my Suranne's face again. Pulling away from my drive I took a quick glance at the dashboard clock.

4:15 p.m.

I would be early, but whatever. Ashley would be happy for the extra time with her, and I'd be happy just being in her presence; anything to get rid of the shitty feeling that was resonating in my damn chest.

I drove quickly, eager to see her again, getting more and more impatient as the minutes ticked by. A sigh of relief escaped me once I pulled into her driveway, but I didn't get the chance to open my door. My cell vibrated and I glanced at the caller id and smiled when I saw it was Suranne.

That smile soon left when I heard her say my name through a heartbreaking sob.

"Suranne?" My heart rate increased, a sense of dread washing over me already. Her hiccupping cries continued through the phone, and then I heard a loud projected voice in the background, announcing information about flights.

Flights.

I would recognize that type of information anywhere.

My girl was at the airport.

She continued crying, occasionally sobbing my name and attempting to push words out. I didn't need them. The sound of her tears told me everything.

"Why the *hell* are you at the airport?" I asked slowly, already knowing the answer, already feeling the pain flooding inside me, the urge to scream out, but unable to stop myself from asking.

"I don't *want to* Kane. Please don't let me go. I don't. I *can't*. I have to leave at six." Her stuttered, watery words caused me to grimace bitterly. I shook my head in denial, although she couldn't see me. I couldn't speak. All I wanted was her. At my place. Eating dinner.

Was that too much to ask?

Why the hell couldn't anything ever work for us, even when we had finally given in to the love we felt for each other?

"I'm sorry, Kane. I—I'm s—so . . ." her sobs stopped her from finishing her sentence, and abruptly, the line disconnected.

Without even thinking, I had reversed out of her drive, hastily putting my car into the highest gear, and speeding, wanting to have my girl in my arms again as quickly as damn possible.

My chest was constricted and tight as hell as I wheezed through a painful exhale. My throat was clogged and my ears were stinging as I weaved through the slow-ass cars that were in my way. I knew I was going twice, possibly even three times the speed limit.

I didn't give a shit.

I needed her to be with me.

I needed her to stay.

Even though I had just been through this shit, I just couldn't imagine making it through several days without her being there, in school, or in my room, or my being in her room. I couldn't imagine not being able to finally kiss her when I wanted to.

I skidded around a corner as the hectic thoughts rushed through my mind, her voice, sobbing over the phone, the voice in the background announcing her boarding time. Six O' Clock.

It was 5:30 p.m. My mind had been such a messy blur, I hadn't realized so much time had passed, or that my windshield and windows were victims of a constant beating rain. I pushed my foot down even further. I had to be close by now.

I knew that her flight would be called and boarded at least fifteen damn minutes before the plane actually took off, taking my girl away from me. That thought alone made me wince in pain and anger.

She couldn't leave.

The sign for the airport came into view, and I thanked the Lord that it was the next exit. I sped through the parking lot, not giving a shit about finding a space, skidding to a stop in the taxi lane. Slamming the door shut I ran for my life, the wind and rain tearing through my hair and slapping at my face as I rushed to get inside. Panting, I looked for the overseas terminal and its separate waiting area where I was sure she would be. Spinning my head round, my eyes trying to find their way through all the bastards with their heavy-ass luggage, I pushed past a couple of people, not even acknowledging them.

And then I spotted it.

Flight 1807 to Gatwick. Departing 6:00 p.m.

I sped for the terminal, noticing the time was 5:40 on the huge clock. My eyes snapped to different directions, desperate to spot her hair, or face, or just *anything* that I would recognize as Suranne. My chest was heaving, my heart pounding erratically. My limbs were burning from the physical exertion, screaming for mercy, but I still didn't give a shit.

I couldn't stop looking.

It was like my eyes grew tunnel vision, and time stood still when I spotted her. My breathing stopped, my heart raced, and everything . . . absolutely *everything* just came crashing back down onto me, the memories, the events, the stress, the tears, the laughter . . . the whispers of "I love you" compared to the punk I was before this girl came into my life.

It all came back.

And in a nanosecond, a *nanosecond*, just like that, it was ripped away from me. The impact of actually seeing her, suitcase in her hand and tears in her eyes, just solidified the turn of events.

It was happening.

She really was leaving.

My body was locked, limbs frozen as I watched her . . . but everything changed when her large gray eyes lifted and came to rest on mine.

Flashes of the different emotions I had seen in those exact gray orbs came to mind; how bright they were when she was happy and when she laughed, how they would burn and darken with passion, or how they would flash when she was angry or in pain.

Her full pink lips parted as she continued staring at me, and I saw her mouth my name.

And then I ran, not giving a shit about the figure standing next to her. Not until I was right in front of her, our bodies mashed together as my arms wound tightly around her waist, did I realize it was her aunt.

She balled the fabric of my shirt into her hands as she sobbed uncontrollably in my chest. Her nose pressed hard against my skin causing my heart to break and feel a little more defeated with each sob. I tightly shut my eyes and buried my face in her hair, for the first time feeling frightened.

Frightened of what I was about to lose.

Frightened of who I'd be when I walked out of this damn building.

Because I could feel it—that dark, cold, uncaring asshole I used to be was rearing his ugly black head again, lurking beneath the surface, just waiting for the final snap, the last push until I would fall over the edge and never resurface.

And I didn't wanna be him again. I had rediscovered what it felt like to be normal. I had lived on the other side, where the grass was much, much greener. And that was where I wanted to goddamn well stay.

It wasn't until I finally pulled away that I noticed my cheeks were wet, and there were tears streaming down my face.

I was crying.

I didn't care.

I tried saying my baby's name.

I couldn't. It was too painful.

"Please don't leave," I managed to choke out through the agony. If I thought three weeks were bad enough without her . . . I couldn't do it.

"Kane," she cried.

I shook my head, pressing my forehead against hers, my hands firmly holding the sides of her face, fingers buried deeply into the wavy locks of her mahogany hair.

"Please. Don't go."

"I *have* to," she wailed loudly, as if begging for me to understand the reasoning. I couldn't. I just *couldn't*.

"No. You don't understand. You can't leave. D'you hear me?" My voice was low, scratchy, a broken record, begging the same thing over and over again. Our lips inched closer every time one of us spoke.

"Kane . . . I—"

I didn't let her finish. I pushed my lips onto hers roughly, snapping my eyes shut and savoring everything about her: her taste, her smell, and the feel of her skin. Saving it to memory and wishing it would never have to go.

Our tears mingled against our connected lips, the saltiness seeping into the kiss and making it bittersweet. The overhead speakers announced her flight and awareness started bleeding back into my head.

It was time for her to go.

I stopped kissing her, but didn't move away. We breathed each other in, our breaths mingling with the tears and the pain and reluctance.

"Please don't go," I whispered against her lips. "You can't leave me."

She merely sobbed in response. Her eyes were defeated, her shoulders were slumped wearily.

There was nothing I could do to stop it.

Her aunt grabbed her arm softly; a gentle reminder that our time was up. I couldn't help but wonder, couldn't help but snicker menacingly at the shitty hand fate had dealt me. Had our whole relationship, the whole thing just been a ticking time bomb?

Suranne's pulling away and grabbing her suitcases gave me the answer.

I stood, numb and unfeeling, as a frail, weak Suranne wheeled her luggage away from me. Standing at the security gate, she gave her aunt a limp hug and a few whispered words before she turned back to me.

Her eyes were dead. Unseeing. Conquered.

But her lips. Her lips moved as she mouthed that she loved me; a silent, unheard whisper that only I would ever appreciate.

I mouthed them back at her.

Because I always would.

She turned again and as her body slowly disappeared from sight, I tightly closed my eyes, and rejoined her in my mind, almost losing myself to the mirage of hopeful happiness that was unraveling in my head. But when I opened them again, only her aunt remained, her back to me as she stood staring at where Suranne had just been.

I turned and left, already feeling the change, and giving into it wholly . . .

Because my life had already left me.

My life had just boarded a plane to Gatwick, London.

I was already dead.

# 38. Memories And A Final Goodbye

## Suzanne

They wouldn't stop.

The tears just wouldn't stop.

My cries had—the painful, aching sobs that had cracked through my ribs and bubbled through my lips like a wounded animal begging to be relieved of its pain.

But the tears still fell. Sliding down the wet trail of my cheek, and dropping onto my jeans. Each drop taking away a memory, a kiss, a smile, an *I love you*.

My body was detoxing, reluctantly preparing itself for the empty, gaping hole inside of me that had been filled by him.

My heart was lying helpless and shattered; its sharp edges jabbed wildly against flesh and bone and sinew.

I lifted the tiny window shade of the plane, knowing that there were only a few feet, some doors, and a counter keeping me from Kane. From the person who completed me.

And there was nothing I could do about it. I had stopped myself from talking to him until I was at the airport, hoping it would make things easier. But it didn't.

The tears continued to fall.

They fell through the whispering bustle as other passengers found their seats and played with the various accessories in random pocket holes.

They fell as an elderly couple glanced at me with worried expressions, then smiled warmly before finding their seats and returning to the bubble of their own lives.

They fell as a slim air hostess crouched down and softly asked me if I was OK, her forehead creased and concerned.

My head nodded.

My heart didn't.

My eyes stayed fixed on where I had just come from. Wishing, praying, begging *someone* that I could just jump up and leave the plane, run into Kane's arms like in one of those films whilst he whirled me around in a tight circle so everything could just go back to being fine.

My limbs felt heavy, too heavy to raise a hand and wipe away the constant moisture on my cheeks. Too heavy to listen to the generic chatter around me. Too heavy to turn my head and comment on the conversation that was happening in the aisle, about how exciting London was going to be.

They would be disappointed.

Or maybe they wouldn't. Whatever.

Maybe it would be everything they ever dreamed of. They would indulge in all of the touristy activities, riding on a roofless bus around town whilst some fat cockney man talked about the various buildings and statues. They would snap pictures and hoot when Big Ben chimed on the hour, every hour, and take videos of the event.

They would try out the national dish upon arrival, humming and nodding, or grimacing and spitting it out.

Whatever they did, it would be an experience. One they would cherish and remember throughout their lives.

For me?

It would be a reminder of everything I had lost.

And everything that I would never gain again.

I sat there, thinking about everything, forcing myself to remember every detail, picking it apart and studying it closely. I didn't want to ever forget.

I thought about the first time I had ever laid eyes on Kane. How the whole class had fallen silent upon his entrance, how I was transfixed with his good looks. The way every girl greeted him as he stalked closer and closer to my desk, a man on a mission.

I felt my lips tug up into a tiny, sad smile as I thought about our first conversation. His condescending, cocky attitude, his soft voice as he spoke about how he was 'The best', and how I had basically insulted what he had in his pants.

Of course, now I knew my statement then was completely innacurate.

I thought back to how I had summed up his psychological problems about his commitment to women during lunch. A laugh escaped me at how much I had actually despised him back then. Hated how he was impossibly gorgeous and yet so frustratingly cocky and irritating.

And yet through all that, I had managed to fall deeply and completely in love with him. The smile still held its place on my lips as I dissected every single memory, reminding myself over and over of what we had.

The tears still fell, tainting the edges of each thought and reminding me of what was lost.

Our first kiss, at two in the morning outside my house.

I smiled when I thought of the morning after, and how he had sauntered down the hallway with his arm over that other girl. I couldn't regret it. If he had never done that, I probably never would've found out about the tragic loss of his father. Remembering that caused me to think about how my being on a plane—the very same machine that had caused Kane such loss—would possibly be affecting him even worse.

A watery laugh bubbled through my lips as I thought about our semi-picnic in the park. Our argument about Beethoven and the meanings underlying the piece.

That brought about the memory of the first time he played the piano for me. The burning emotion in his eyes afterwards, and how it led to such a passionate afternoon, giving me feelings I never even knew were possible.

Did I know that I loved him then?

I had definitely felt something.

I forced myself to think about the darker times. My feelings of doubt when I found about his history with Kate. The guilt when I had decided to leave with her instead of him.

That dark night, the anniversary of his father's death. The unfamiliar look in his eyes that had instilled such fear within me. Yet I had stayed until my declaration of love for him wasn't returned.

That thought only spurred me to remember when it finally was returned. How the setting had been so perfect, the song, the history of the building, and the feel of his warm arms around my waist as we swayed to the music.

And of course, the tie.

I had to laugh at his common use of expletives, remembering how he would randomly swear about such inconsequential things. I remembered how I used to tease him about his short temper and impatience with inanimate objects. How he would shrug, as if it was just the way things were.

A wistful sigh escaped my chest as I finally lifted my hand; wiping at the tears as the flight attendant announced our depature.

I felt the gentle vibration of the plane moving; there was no going back. The runway passed by outside the window, the airport separating itself from me with every second.

I couldn't see the end of the runway, but I could feel it disappearing behind us, every inch of the grey tarmac tearing away at me, removing itself from my presence and everything that I had achieved here. And then we were airborne; the final string connecting me to this country, to the grass and the road and the school, was cut loose as soon as the wheels folded beneath the large machine and it relied on its wings and engines to lift itself into the air, mingling with the dark clouds and sky.

I whispered a final goodbye as I saw the runway become smaller, the airport decrease in size, removing itself further from my grasp. A final goodbye to my aunt, to my home for the last three months, to the school, to Kate, to Lawrence . . .

The tears made a silent appearance once again.

Closing my eyes, I rested my head back against the seat and whispered a final goodbye to Kane Richards—and the love I would probably never see again . . .

# 39. Epilogue

## Kane

Two months.

Two fucking months.

I took a deep breath and grimaced as the familiar, aching pain still burned in my chest. But that shit was nothing new. I'd been having that goddamn pain for two long, shitty months now. I was used to it. I almost embraced it. It proved to me that I was not going to forget her. That I still loved her, and that she was real.

A light knock brought my attention to the here and now, and I stared at the door, waiting for it to open. I knew it would; they never bothered waiting for a response from me anymore. They knew they would be waiting forever if they did.

My mom poked her head through and smiled sadly at me.

"Hey, honey," she murmured softly. I gave her a halfhearted nod and stared back at the blue screen on my TV. It had been like that for about a week. I couldn't be bothered with turning it off. It was a miracle I even left my damn room at all. In fact, I only ever did when my stomach screamed out in protest, demanding that I feed myself.

"Pretty big day today, huh?" she asked. I frowned as I remembered she was in my room. Recently, I had developed some kind of short-term memory loss; sometimes going to the toilet and not even remembering getting up, or even needing to go in the first place. If I was at school, which I hadn't been lately, I would be listening to one of my teachers droning on one minute, and then the next I would be in the cafeteria, sitting at the same table I'd sat at when she was here. Except now, it held only one.

"Yeah," I rasped, my voice rough from the lack of use. To be honest I really didn't give a shit about today. I hadn't given a shit about any day recently. There was only one thing I wanted. One thing I needed, and guess what?

She was thousands of miles away. Tucked up in *London*, doing everything that made her beautiful when she was around me. The last we talked, she told me that her mom was doing better. It was good just hearing the sound of her voice, but that didn't change the fact that she'd left.

"Kane," I heard my mom sigh as she crossed the room and sat on the end of my bed. "This has to stop, baby. I know you miss h—"

I threw my palm up to stop her.

"Don't even mention her name," I hissed sharply. I didn't want her name to pass my mother's lips. I didn't want her name to be spoken by *anyone* except me. She was mine and no matter what, she always would be. I tightly shut my eyes, imagining myself years from now without her. Would I still have this same shitty ache? Would I still be dreaming of her endlessly at night? Would I ever be the same again without her?

For some reason I couldn't picture myself in the future alone. The images just wouldn't come, and after a while I just gave up with a frustrated and weary sigh.

My mom once again reminded me that she was still in my damn room. I flinched when she rested her hand on my knee, not used to having anyone touch me. I brought my hands up to tug at my hair.

Today was graduation, and regardless of how messed up I was, I needed to go.

I cleared my throat and rubbed a palm over my face roughly. "Let me get dressed," I mumbled digging the heel of my hands into my eyes.

"OK," my mom replied, and squeezed my knee gently before getting up to leave my room. I watched her sadly; she still hadn't touched a drink and she deserved to be told how proud I was of her, like I had done before. But after all the shit that had been going down, I just hadn't really thought about it.

My mom turned around just before she reached for the door. "I know you're hurting right now. I'm sorry." She smiled warmly and was about to shut the door behind her before I called out to her,

"Mom, I . . ." I sighed and turned my face back to the blue TV screen. "I'm proud of you," I muttered into the silent space between us. I didn't feel the need to look back at her, and after a moment, I heard the soft click of my door closing, signaling she had left.

\*\*\*

"Hey man, wait up!"

I recognized that voice and closed my eyes. I just wanted to get this over and *done* with, didn't want to have congratulatory conversations or 'no hard feeling' talks. In the past few months, I thought people had understood in this damn school not to approach me. It was weird how my status had completely changed. Girls would still give me side glances, sometimes being brave enough to approach me, trying to "ease my pain."

I would tell them to back the hell off.

Apart from that, the whole time at school had passed in a mind-numbingly plain blur. A month ago was my eighteenth birthday.

Something that, before Suranne had come into my life, I had planned to be a huge event.

That plan went to shit.

I stayed in my room that night, drinking Grey Goose straight and holding my head in my hands, begging for just five minutes of calmness, just five minutes where I wouldn't have to deal with the image of her constantly burning behind my eyelids. Just five minutes away from the damn stinging tears.

It never happened. That night, and every night after that, I curled up in the same position, sighing in relief when the burn of the alcohol and the blank numbing mask it provided finally pulled over my body and carried me toward bittersweet nothingness.

"Yo! Kane! Wait up!" Lawrence's out-of-breath voice brought me back to the school, the crowd of students, shrouded in our stupid-ass robes and hats and our proud parents finding chairs anticipating their child's five seconds of fame when they would step up on that stage. They would shake the valedictorian's sweaty hand before climbing back down those steps, blending back into the sea of plain faces, each one carrying a different future, a different path leading them on to the next chapter of their life.

I knew because pretty soon, I would be one of those students.

I turned with a weary sigh to face Lawrence only a few feet away from me, his arm slung firmly over a slender unfamiliar girl with a bronze complexion and dark hair.

I raised an eyebrow at Lawrence questioningly. Apparently I had missed quite a bit these couple of months.

He picked up on my questioning stare and smiled proudly down at the girl as she clutched at his waist tightly. She looked at me appraisingly, her eyes raking over my form, but surprised me when she just turned back to Lawrence, kissing him on the cheek and whispering something in his ear.

And for the first time ever I saw Lawrence blush.

She walked off then, leaving just the two of us. He stared at me, with a newfound maturity and an expression of mild concern.

"What is it?" I asked simply, my voice scratchy and devoid of emotion.

Lawrence sighed and looked down at the ground as he toed the grass with his shoe before lifting his head back up to face me. He opened his mouth to say something, but closed it just as quickly; copying the same movement over and over, until I felt irritation flare within me.

"Will you just *spit it out* already?"

"It's nothing," he sighed and turned to walk away, but stopped himself short to face me again, his face determined. "I just wanted to say . . . Good luck, y'know. With everything, and whatever you decide to do after . . . *this*." He waved his hand around us, and I followed it, noticing my Mom watching me warily from her seat.

I nodded and sighed, turning to walk away towards Mom, but he stopped me again.

"Kane, also . . . I'm sorry." He looked at me firmly; his apology was genuine and I knew he was apologizing for everything with her.

"Thanks," I muttered, nodding my head again. He gave a small smile and turned, walking towards the girl waiting for him by the chairs. I watched her curiously, noticed how her face brightened and a smile graced her lips as she saw him approaching her.

"Lawrence!" I called out to him, and he paused, turning around with a curious expression on his face.

"Congratulations," I nodded my head towards the girl, admitting to actually being happy that he had found someone. His face morphed into a grin, and he nodded back at me before going back to his girl.

I wished I could go back to mine.

Graduation thankfully passed fairly quickly. Girls were crying and hugging each other, guys were clapping each other's shoulders in congratulations while their parents mingled and gushed about how proud they were of their kids.

My mom being one of them.

I watched her silently, focusing on her reactions and facial expressions. She talked with a bright glint in her eyes, and her soft feminine laugh carried out into the hall and warmed me every time. I could feel my resolve hardening, solidifying in my brain and putting itself into action.

I carried on watching her silently, until my eyes found Ashley. She lifted her head and looked at me, her gaze warming as her face split into the wide grin that I loved, her eyes bright and gleaming. I savored her smile, keeping it firmly locking in my memory as I slipped out of the hall. An eerie calm washed over my body, flowing through my blood as it began repairing my heart and gearing it back into action. I drove home in silence, watching the road thoughtfully, studying each line of the pavement and other cars as they passed me and turned off onto different roads, wondering where they would take them.

I turned into my driveway and entered the living area. As I approached the stairs, I brushed my hand along the soft wood of the railings before walking into my room and sitting on my bed. I looked at the piano thoughtfully, admiring the sleek black exterior and the gold-outlined planes.

The next hour passed in a blur, my body so calm and my movements so fluid that I hardly registered what I was doing before I finished. I walked to the door of my room and turned, remembering the space. I continued to smile as I walked down the stairs and into the kitchen, placing the necessary things on the table for when Mom got home. A short time later, I walked out the front door and settled into the smooth leather seat of my car. I sighed at the purr of the engine and drove, my lips still turned upward into that calm smile, my body completely relaxed and at ease with acceptance.

And then I was there, walking into the building with all those memories, I squinted at the bright lights but carried on walking, never wavering till I reached the appropriate area.

I stopped, my body at a standstill, as a woman watched me curiously, her eyebrow quirked and her lips set into a tight line. I felt a flicker of hesitation, but it passed quickly and I was flooded once again with unwavering calmness as I carried on moving forward. The woman's face changed into the polite smile required to greet everyone. That was, after all, her job.

"Good afternoon, Sir. What can I help you with today?"

I closed my eyes and drew in a deep breath, nodding to myself, knowing this was the right thing to do.

Because after two months of pain, I still loved Suranne more than ever. And because wherever the hell she went, I would damn well make sure that I would follow.

Opening my eyes, I gazed at the woman and smiled politely back at her, opening my mouth and giving the one sentence that would change my future entirely.

"First class, one-way ticket to Gatwick, London."

# Acknowledgments

There are a lot of people without whose help and support this book wouldn't have been possible. I would like to thank my copyeditor, Kelly Lenox, and my book designer, Kimberly Martin, for their awesome work on my book.

I want to thank my family and friends for their support and constant praise, especially my brothers and my Mum. I'd also like to thank Lisa Paul, my publisher. She had faith in my story when I thought no one else would.

And of course, the fans, which I gained through the early stage of writing this book. Also, I'd like to thank you, the reader, for taking an interest in my book. It means a lot!